CONSUMMATION OF
NEMA

Written by
Iriel Sayeed

irielsayeed@hotmail.com

©2017 Iriel Sayeed

DEDICATION

This book is dedicated to my Creator, Thee God of my understanding. Thanks for being my everything and gifting me with this story! I prayed so long for a novel of my own, Thank you Universe.

I would like to thank my parents and friends for encouraging me and always asking about the book. I won't name names but I hold everyone of you in my heart. Much love for your support and love always!

I would also like to thank Layla Livingston for being my first character. A poet at heart I prayed for this story for a long time. Layla pushed me through whenever I got stuck and she was sad when the story ended.

I would like to thank my editor Myki Bobo!!! For pushing me to complete this project! Thanks for the love, encouragement and support we'll build more things together!!! Love you to life Sister.

Dear Reader,

This book is my heaven and afterlife in words. I put everything I've learned traveling and exploring in these pages.

My editor and myself did our best to translate the book as accurate as possible, please excuse any grammatical errors, we were on our own in a world of Dutch (which I speak, but can't write), Swahili and Spanish. I wanted my story to be colored with different dialects and diversity.

This novel has been my love child for many years and I hope you can feel the passion and effort I poured into it with each word you read!

I hope you enjoy the adventure, and the story as much as I did writing it!

Peace

TABLE OF CONTENTS

CHAPTER ONE: LAYLA

Layla awoke to the sweet sounds of Robin Thicke singing 'Sex in the Morning' on her cell phone alarm clock. Reaching over she squeezed the sides of her phone with one hand and rolled back over onto her right side, facing the only window in her room and the love of her life.

Staring at Robert in his sleep Layla fell in love with him all over again. She felt the electric pull towards him since they met at her neighborhood church five years ago. He walked into her life and became her best friend and protector.

Scooting over, Layla decided to take her ringtones advice and initiate some of her own 'sex in the morning'.

She licked her lips and began kissing his neck, sucking on his left ear. He stirred a bit, still faking sleep. She caressed his chest with her tongue, dipping the tip into his navel. When he rolled over onto his back, she knew she had his attention.

Licking the tip of 'the lil boss', that was their nick-name for his most invaluable body part, going round and around with her tongue. He put his hands in her hair. Upon hearing him moan, she swallowed all of him, the tip of his penis grazing her wisdom teeth. Holding him in her mouth she hummed slowly, moving her head up and down to her own secret melody.

She continued to suck him until he raised his knees and lifted her head to face him. Kissing her he pulled her on top of him into a sitting position in his lap. Positioning himself inside her she rode him cow girl style as he slammed his hips into her rising legs, meeting each accompanied thrust. Climaxing simultaneously, moaning aloud in unison sealing their love with a kiss.

"Good morning baby!" smiled Robert in response to Layla's wake me up.

"I know how you like waking up to love in the morning" grinned Layla.

"Better than coffee!" laughed Robert.

"My caffeine dream/I burst at the seams/soul redeemed/you're so supreme!" chanted Robert and Layla laughing at one of the number of poems Robert recites in honor of them.

"I have to use the rest room doll" states Robert standing, kissing Layla on the forehead before he exists.

Layla watched his tall slender brown bottom and smiled. He was so sexy with his muscular body and short dreadlocks. She could have sworn 'lil boss' winked as he left the room.

Wrapping herself in their soft white comforter and sheet, Layla stretched out in their California King Bed.

Gazing out into the street she remembered where she was...Cincinnati Ohio! Layla was born and raised in this city she despised. Coming into consciousness at the ripe age of sixteen, she experienced the racism her city breeds.

Born to Oscar Livingston, a real estate mogul and Inez Garcia Livingston a RN, she was exposed to travelling, living abroad in Spain with relatives during the summer, family reunions in different states every two years. Layla knew that other cities provided a place for not only black people, but all humans to relax. Chicago has Lake Shore, New York has city blocks and Amsterdam has Wester Park!

She couldn't smoke weed in Eden Park in Cincinnati like she could on the stairs of Lake Shore in Chicago. She didn't see black and Latinos in high positions in Cincinnati like she did in New York or Cali and being from both cultures she felt the animosity from both ends.

Cincinnati was full of crime and nice places to be, the people must come to an understanding, stop being so conservative, because whenever you see a cluster of black people, the police were not far behind! She had to get out of this city! Yet at twenty, Layla knew where ever you go, there you are! Another city was just another place to survive! Something was missing from her life! She had to put her finger on it!

"Hey babe, what would you like for breakfast? Waffles or bagels?" asked Robert sticking his head into the room, breaking into Layla's thoughts.

"A bagel with peanut butter and I'll roll a blunt" answered Layla sitting up to prepare for their daily rituals.

Both Robert and Layla remained naked, Layla pulled out their marijuana and proceeded to roll a spliff in their bedroom as Robert prepared breakfast in the kitchen.

Rolling the sweet ganja the streets called 'loud' expertly inside an emptied silver white owl cigar, Layla got off the bed and continued into the dining area.

Layla and Robert occupied a pent house in the Kenwood area of the city. Her father being in real estate, was her landlord, she paid him when she wanted, between two hundred and nothing a month. She took the seven hundred Robert gave her each month for bills and spent it on clothes and shoes.

Robert was twenty seven and worked as an up and coming 'game maker' for GEMS a toy company whose biggest competitor was Fisher Price. He had just developed a child proofing technique that would be patented by the company and make him a wealthy man! He was lucky that his job only drug tested during orientation, so he had no fear of random screenings.

Assisting her mother at the Westside's outpatient center, Layla felt rewarded helping others. While studying nursing at UC, she and her mother correlated care for seven individuals residing in a nursing home environment. Looking forward to becoming a nurse like her mother, she studied long, wrote poetry about her life and partied hard whenever she had the chance.

Sitting at their dining room table, Layla observed Robert slicing fruit in the kitchen. He smiled at her as she inhaled the joint she rolled.

"Turn on some music" commanded Robert walking to the table with the fruit and bagels on separate plates in each hand.

Layla did as she was asked, standing she pushed back the chair she was sitting in, one of the four silver iron chairs that encased their glass table. Turning right she padded over the beige shag carpet to their stereo, hitting 'play' "Compass" by Vybz Kartel began to play.

She began dancing around the room, skipping back into the dining area, she kissed Robert and handed him the joint. Taking a bite of her bagel, she lovingly sat across from him, swallowing before speaking.

"I have to shower; I'll finish my bagel when I get out. Are you still meeting me downtown for Jason's exhibit today?" questioned Layla.

"Yes! I wouldn't miss my little brother's show for the world! What time does it start? Eight?" inquired Robert.

"Seven, I'll come home around five to freshen up! Mom doesn't need my help and I only have a few errands, so I'll get home and leave around six and meet you there!" explained Layla.

"Alright! Sounds like a plan, I should be off around five. I sign the patent today!" gushed Robert.

"Yay! Baby I couldn't be prouder!" smiled Layla.

"I live to make you proud!" expressed Robert pulling her towards him into an embrace.

Layla was very appreciative for all that Robert provided. Their two bedrooms was filled with lovely things, all black leather furniture in the living room, African masks enriched the walls, state of the art electronics adorned all rooms from the ninety five inch flat screen in their sitting room to the appliances in the kitchen.

Yet it was more than the materialistic things that Robert provided. He was her soul mate, the team mate Thee Creator made for her, she was his prime rib!

***

As the warm water sprouted down around her, Layla tried to pin point that burning sensation in her belly. She began to reflect....

Living an ample lifestyle, her 4.0 GPA was effort enough for her parents to provide her every whim. Going to the nursing home and paying her father a couple of dollars here and there was the icing on the cake!

Just like when she attended grade school, one hundred dollars for every A and fifty for every B. Now every year she's in nursing school her parents agreed to dispense her allowance that covered her entire lifestyle. Paying her father a little rent money demonstrated independence.

With the money she received from her parents, school and Robert, Layla had her every need met. Whatever one didn't cover the other would and with three solid resources of cash, Layla had no intentions of working a nine to five anytime soon!

There is more to life than studying, fucking and dancing! At twenty she had her entire life in front of her. In college Layla became conscious of her environment and her fragility there in.

Layla had her financial aspect of life under control. She didn't really want to become a nurse but felt following in her mother's steps was the right thing to do. She relished in the rewarding feeling that accompanied caring for others. It was a reminder of how blessed she was to be of sound mind and body. Yet, in her reflecting she found that she had no true aspirations of her own.

Turning off the water, Layla stepped onto the terry cloth towel that protected her tile floor and began to dry off. Caressing her brown skin, she wrapped the towel around her and proceeded to exit the restroom.

Opening the door she bumped into Robert, who was standing in the hallway anticipating her return.

Not saying a word, Robert kissed her as she wrapped her arms around his neck. Her towel tumbled to the floor.

Pushing her against the wall, Robert continued to assault her with his lips. Sliding down her neck, ears and chest with his tongue, Layla began to moan and slide down the wall.

Lifting her into his arms, Robert held Layla over his head, performing oral sex mid air!

Layla squealed in delight! Fearing he would drop her and the thrill of his tongue on her sex drove her wild.

"Robert" she whined, the feeling becoming too much to endure.

Robert complied by licking her one last hard time from back to front. Stopping to nibble at her clitoris, he lowered her down, perforating her being with his penis.

"Shit" gasped Layla

Robert began to pump in and out of Layla slowly, stopping to carry her to their bedroom. He continued to make love to Layla standing up. Grabbing his shoulders and throwing her head back, Layla enjoyed the ride!

Slowing down his pace, Robert eased out of Layla, setting her on her feet.

"Spread your legs and grab your ankles!" Robert ordered salaciously.

Confronting the lust in his eyes, Layla spread her thighs and complied.

Robert dropped to his knees and proceeded to lick Layla like a lollipop. She moaned and her legs began to tremble. Just when she could take no more and was about to beg him to stop, he did. Grabbing her hips and entering her from behind.

Slowly he penetrated Layla, gradually picking up the tempo. His hips moved to their own rhythm, as their bodies clapped together, the noise made Layla wetter. Exploding around his 'lil boss', they both cried out, collapsing onto their bed.

Spooning, his front to her back, Layla smiled, trying to catch her breath.

"I have to shower" Robert stated kissing Layla on the cheek and easing out of her gently. He stood, stretched and yawned before exiting the bedroom.

Layla smiled, wrapped up in the thought of him. He filled her like no other, probing her temple, pleasuring her physique and bemusing her core.

She praised the Most High for placing them together. Meeting Robert at St. Paul's Baptist was a blessing and a moment she will never forget.

Layla being an only child, loved to shadow her mother,

they were
close friends. It had been a couple of months since Layla
had attended service and she promised her mother she
would visit that following
Sunday, Mother's Day.

Under no circumstance will she forget smelling marijuana
upon entering
the sanctuary. Turning to her right she noticed a beautiful
brown skin brother sitting next to an older woman, bearing
a strong resemblance,
Layla assumed she was his mother. He reeked of weed! In
church of all places! Layla and her mother sat in the pews
directly in front of him,
near the rear of the building. The singing was magnetic
and Layla
enjoyed herself, loving that the words to the songs were
projected on
a screen above the choir, making it easy to sing along.

It was the pastor's sermon that brought Layla and Robert
together. The reverend spoke about unity and everyone
being one. He then went on to contradict himself and say
that homosexuals were going to hell!
Apparently Layla and Robert both disagreed, standing at
the same time,
as if on queue, they both proceeded to retreat, neither
giving
explanations to their mothers.

Walking behind him, Layla could visualize their love
making. He was so

tall, 6'5 she guessed, later she was informed he was 6'7!
She
followed him through the foyer of the house of God into the
parking lot.
He turned and addressed her once they were outside; she
knew he
knew she stayed behind him. Not diverting to speak to the
many
guests that called to her, Layla simply nodded, keeping
close behind Robert.
"Wanna smoke a joint?" was Robert's first question.

As she inhaled she could not fathom smoking ganja on
God's property!
Thee Creator was everything. As she inhaled Thee Creator
in the form of some of the purest weed into her lungs on
that day, she praised Jehovah
as the weed smoke united them.

They discussed their disagreement with the pastor's
judgment. Bonding
in their connection to allow others to live and love as they
choose.
Robert was so clairvoyant and open minded, he said "If
God didn't
want same sex relationships he wouldn't have created a
choice. He
would never put something here on earth for us to
experience to
turn around and punish us for experiencing it!"

She was impressed by his intelligence and how comfortable

he
was with himself.

"Boo" whispered Robert into Layla's ear, putting an end to her musing.

"Remember smoking that joint in the church parking lot?" asked Layla allowing Robert into her thoughts.

"Can't forget! Been high on you every day since lover!" exclaimed Robert smiling, exposing his perfect teeth encased by thick brown lips Layla loved to suck.

"Yeah, I love being with you" Layla.

"But?" Robert questioned.

"No, but" answered Layla.

"I hear something else in your voice" Robert stated, rubbing lotion into his skin, Layla wanted to do that for him.

"Its not you, not us" she said instead of assisting him with his personal care, admiring Robert's ability to be in tuned to her deepest desires.

"Well?" inquired Robert pulling a shirt over his damp hair.

"I'm happy; I just feel something is amiss, astray." Explained Layla.

"Amiss? Astray? What, we speaking in poetry now?" laughed Robert.

"Funny! I just feel something is missing!" Layla.

"Umm…you working?" giggled Robert.

"Don't! Work is *NOT* all there is! And I know what I want to do with my life career wise. However, there is this feeling in the pit of my stomach that says I should be doing something more! I just don't know what that *something* is." clarified Layla.

"Could it be…Making more love to me?" asked Robert with an obscene gleam in his eye. Layla smiled, pursing her lips, it was hard to stay upset with a man full of lyrical rebuttals!

"No!" laughed Layla.

"Could it be... Cooking more?" laughed Robert, dodging a pillow Layla tossed his way in response to his teasing.

"It's time for you to go to work!" squealed Layla running around the bed as Robert chased her. Catching her he tossed her up in the air, spinning her around he said "We will figure out this yearning of yours together" After kissing her passionately he threw her onto the bed!

***

Layla was happy she only had three classes today. Almost dozing off in anatomy, she blamed her drowsiness on the weed!

Lunch couldn't come fast enough and sharing a meal with Tracy was always a treat! Tracy Millen had been Layla's best friend since third grade, meeting on their Silverton elementary playground. Her candid observation of all she encountered kept Layla in fits of laughter every time they spent time together. Today would be no different, smiled Layla to herself, waving to Tracy as they walked towards one another.

"Hey lady" greeted Layla kissing Tracy on the cheek Dutch style(three kisses)

"Hey purple rain!" grinned Tracy in return, commenting on Layla's purple jumpsuit and platforms.

"You silly, how was chemistry? Did you see Brian, Ryan, Zion, Crying" laughed Layla.

"Stop stupid" giggled Tracy in her 'Wendy Williams, how you doing?' voice. "Yes he was there looking sexy and studious!" concluded Tracy playfully shoving Layla's shoulder.

"OOOH! Were you lab mates?" questioned Layla.

"No, Professor Lame Nuts lectured on atoms and the physical reactions inside cells, while I studied the back of Brian's 'please be mine' Banks head" sighed Tracy.

"He'll ask you out! He'll tap into yawl's *chemistry*" smirked Layla.

"He better, or he'll miss out on all this!" stated Tracy making a hideous face, both girls broke out laughing.

"Will you come with me tonight to Jason's exhibit? He's a multifaceted artist that shall be reckon with my dear!" Layla said in her best British accent once their laughter subsided.

"Is he sexy?" asked Tracy in a southern drawl.

"Sistah, he's a sight to see and his craft is a creation to behold" answered Layla.

"Well you are dating his brother, the apple couldn't fall far from that Mandingo tree!" quipped Tracy chuckling she continued "Let's eat!" she said pointing towards the 'Cactus Pear' their favorite café in the city.

After a lunch of laughter with Tracy, Layla finished school and headed to her favorite shop for something to wear that evening to the exhibit.

Nordstrom's had everything Layla needed from the accessories to the shoes.

After purchasing a black knee length dress, embedded with black roses that formed ruffles around the neck, Layla was satisfied, electing to wear some shoes she had at home that would complete the ensemble. Checking her watch as she grabbed some jewelery at a consignment shop she felt like a quick joint in the woods before heading home and dressing for the exposition.

***

An invasion of purple as she exited her black BMW Z6

convertible, smiling at the male to her right eating lunch at a nearby picnic table, she twisted her waist length dreadlocks into a ponytail before walking the path that entered the woods.

Once deep in the forest, Layla found a nice spot and lit her joint. She smoked and watched nature, observing her surroundings, loving the feel of the ganja calming her senses. Her mind wandering to the banal classes she had to endure. She jumped hearing a squirrel rustling in the leaves.

After finishing her joint she sat for awhile more enjoying her high and the atmosphere. Robert didn't like the idea of her being in the forest alone. He was paranoid, concluded Layla, though she had to admit his disapproving of her being there is what drew her to it more.

Then that 'feeling' gripped her gut! That high hollow inkling of mislaid efficiency, she had been battling with this intense sense of unexecuted mirth. For a woman who had it all, from a materialistic aspect, her soul screamed for more! She had to cure this craving, like fat kids love cake, publishing her purpose was her conquest!

Layla came out of her head and sank deeper into her the environment. She felt as high as the sky, stretching her arms as if to touch it she stood. She began her trek back out to her car, when a bad thought ran through her mind; '*Something is going to make you want to run out of here!*' She quickened her pace, thinking about the errands she had to run before returning home. She saw some birds in the grass and stopped.

Suddenly a doe ran across her path sprinting deeper into the forest. Layla stood startled! When she resumed walking she noticed a giant weed stalk. It wasn't there before and it was blocking her exit from the woods! The stalk was enormous! It took up the entire path; its leaves reaching up and out as far as she could see. The leaves blocked out all sunlight. Where were the other trees? Layla noticed this stalk had taken the place of the other smaller trees that aligned the trail.

How could she get out of the park with this ginormous stalk of weed in the way. Layla knew the ganja she consumed was high grade but this was ridiculous! Layla walked up to the stalk and placed her hand on its leaves. The stalk opened up and swallowed Layla whole!

Layla was falling! Her stomach was dropping, arms flailing, heart palpitating! She felt as if she had fallen off of a cliff. She fell and fell, only seeing darkness at first, then she began to see images flash like someone was taking a picture, though she couldn't see where they came from in this tunnel of darkness she was falling through.

Visions of places, people, beings and objects flickered and fizzled before she could decipher what she was seeing. Layla squealed, cursed and prayed before bouncing like a rag doll! As her fall lost its momentum she stopped, ricocheting around the room.

The space was empty, decorated in black, red, gold and green checkered floors, ceilings and walls. Layla looked around the room. There were no doors, no windows, only a wooden coffee table that sat in the middle of the floor with a bottle a top it with the word 'Drenk' written on the label. Where was the table when she was bouncing around the room? Layla wondered, perplexed she checked herself for bruises from the fall. Feeling no soreness and seeing no blood, Layla thought she was fine.

Layla ran around the chamber! Banging on the cushioned walls, jumping on the trampoline like floor, touching the ceiling at times. Layla had to have screamed, cried and smacked the walls for over ten seconds before she even considered the bottle!

Staring at the label for several minutes reading the red letters on the black bottle, Layla opened the container and smelled the contents. It smelled like cherries. Was drinking it her only way out? What does it contain? What is happening? Why is it happening? Maybe it was time to put the weed down! These thoughts ran through Layla's brain simultaneously.

Finding no way out she opened the bottle intending to take a sip. But the cool thick liquid was so tasty she drank the entire bottle. It tasted as it smelled, like cherries and slid down her throat, coating her soul it seemed as it went down. Before she could place the empty bottle on the table she began shrinking! Layla screamed! She said 'God', hoping he would stop the shrinking like he broke her fall, but she continued to get smaller and smaller.

She felt her jumpsuit was smothering her, when she stopped deflating, she had to climb her way out of the jumper. Grabbing hold to the fabric she pulled and climbed to the top, moving towards the light. She reached the top and did a mixture of tumbling, rolling and sliding until she reached the bottom.

A miniature version of herself, Layla ripped a piece of the material tying the fabric around her neck she created a dress to cover her nakedness, looking down she realized she was three feet tall. She felt as if she was losing her mind! Where was the reasoning in what was happening to her? She screamed and she cried monumental waterfall, faucet running tears. She felt like she would drown in her own lamentations if she didn't stop crying but she couldn't help herself. The more she cried the more she felt like crying. Before she knew it she was floating! She grabbed onto the bottle she had drank from, now small enough to use it as a floating devise. She floated to the ceiling and right before her head touched the top, her tears began receding. She slowly winded down to the floor like a child's toy in a bath tub.

Layla was eerily quiet, taking in all that was happening to her. She rolled off the bottle and stood up. There was light pouring into the once windowless room. Layla noticed an oval shaped door and a *Half Rabbit... Half Man* standing there!

"Jambo! mevrouw, Ik ben Hoot A Gin of Rastaland!" said the Rabbit Man doing a little jig.

He had rabbit ears and a fury man face, his upper torso was male but fury. He had rabbit legs and feet, his fur was black his tail was red at the base, green in the middle and gold at the end. He wore a Rasta colored hat, jacket and boots.

"What is happening?" Layla replied in tears.

"Right you speak English!" said Hoot A Gin

"What is happening? Who are you? What do you speak? What did you say?" questioned Layla who was beside herself with fear and anguish.

"One inquiry at a time my dear, What's happening is you've just returned to Rastaland to reign in your rightful place! I am Hoot A Gin of Rastaland, but you can call me Rasta Rabbit. I didn't know what country you were coming from, we speak all languages here. Jambo! is Hi in Swahili, Mervrouw is Dutch for Mrs. or woman and Ik ben is Dutch for I am. So I said: Hi Miss, I am Hoot A Gin of Rastaland! That answered all your questions. You asked what I say and what I speak, to me that's the same question" explained Rasta Rabbit or Hoot A Gin, he pronounced it hoot-again.

Layla giggled "I'm in Rastaland as in Wonderland?

"As in La-la land, the motherland and the promise land! Rastaland is where you are, welcome back your highness" he bowed and continued holding up a finger to stop Layla before she could part her lips with her next question. "Let me explain, you are in another dimension my dear! A place between nowhere and everywhere! You couldn't have thought that Earth was the only civilization God created! Silly Rabit tricks are for kids!" Rasta Rabbit laughed at his joke and Layla's flabbergasted expression before going on "Rastaland is beautiful and you will see and learn more soon. But we must hurry, we have been under attack for sometime and you're a vital key to unlocking the arms of peace. I am happy, so happy that you have returned! The White Witch Winter's reign has turned our once placid vicinity into a frigid village! The Winter Witch is as cold as her name. But before I tell you anymore, before you ask another question, we must leave. I will sprinkle some diminutive dust on your head so that you will fit in my pocket until we cross into the south. You must trust me Layla. I would never harm you!" concluded Rasta Rabbit

Well, Layla thought, he is all I have. His eyes looked sincere and she'd always been a good judge of character. And she just survived almost drowning in her own tears, drank a shrinking potion and been sucked into a weed stalk! What else could go wrong? Could this place be the solution to that yearning in her belly? She cleared her throat "You say I must trust you and I'm so bewildered right now with all that's happening! If more danger is approaching, please promise to take care of me. I have to trust you"

"No worries dear, I have already given my word to serve and protect you forever!" Rasta Rabbit replied bowing again.

He had a familiar calm about him that allowed her to trust him like she did her boyfriend Robert. As a matter of fact, minus the feet and fur Rasta Rabbit reminded her of Robert! Putting those concepts aside she concentrated on the task at hand. And pondered what all Rastaland had in store for her!

CHAPTER TWO: RASTALAND

Rasta Rabbit pulled a golden transparent container from his jacket pocket. The contents looked like sand. Pinching a small amount from the bottle, he proceeded to sprinkle the sandy contents onto the top of Layla's head. She immediately shriveled into a pocket size version of herself. Layla gasped as Rasta Rabbit gently picked her up and placed her into his front jacket pocket. Once she was settled, able to stand inside of his pocket and looking over the bridge of the spongy material, the Rabbit took off at break neck speed.

Rastaland blazed by Layla's eyes, as she tried to keep her balance and take in her new surroundings. She saw different colorful birds, bugs, animals and beings she couldn't identify in the sky and on the ground. The vault of heaven was white with big yellow clouds. And the air would change from ice cold to extremely hot in seconds. Layla found herself shivering and sweating at the same time while trapped in Rasta Rabbits pocket.

Someone yelled: "Hoot!" and Rasta Rabbit came to an abrupt stop. Layla, remained hidden in the jackets material, peered out carefully to see who or why Rasta Rabbit had stopped so suddenly.

"Halt Hoot!" yelled a deep voice. It sounded as if he had rocks in his throat.

Layla peeped over the pocket edge her eyes taking in the sites of a half man half lizard! His upper half was lizard and his lower half human, though his feet were flat and webbed like a ducks. He drooled as he spoke, his partner looked like his twin and they both wore iron helmets with white feathers running down the middle and iron vest, their gigantic hands held machetes.

"Wat doe je hier konijn? (*What are you doing here rabbit?)*", asked the slobbering lizard man.

"Jambo! jongens, Ik ben boos op Zatchel, ik zie hem niet", (*Hey boys, I am mad at Zatchel, I don't see him*), explained Rasta Rabbit.

"Het laatste wat ik zag Zatchel was gisteren of zo, maar dit is niet de plek voor jou!", (*The last I saw Zatchel was yesterday or so, but this is not the place for you*), warned the drooling lizard man.

"Ik weet het, maar ik moet proberen, moet ik vind Zatchel eerste of de King van Rastaland zal echt boos!", (*I know, but I must try, I must find Zatchel first or the King of Rastaland will be really mad*), exclaimed Rasta Rabbit.

Layla heard a wagon approaching from the rear. She went all the way to the corner of the jacket pocket, witnessing a chariot that was ablaze. She watched the repulsive guards stiffen.

"Hoot, je moet nu vertrekken! Maar kom heir noit weer!" (*Hoot, you must leave now! But come here never again!*), yelled the austere lizard man.

Rasta Rabbit saluted before taking off again. Layla hadn't comprehended a word of the conversation, but from Rasta Rabbit's response it was bad. He began sweating dashing off, Layla gripped the jacket's material tighter fearing she would be catapulted from the pocket!

Rasta Rabbit sprinted deeper into the forest that was Rastaland. It seemed like forever to Layla who regarded the Rabbit yelling to birds and talking to the trees that hid them along their journey. When Rasta Rabbit stopped again, Layla saw a castle that towered over the city. It sat inside a mountain with other smaller towers attached to it.

The fortress was black with white designs and painted masks along the upper roofs and down the sides. All of the gates, doors and bridges were red, gold, and green. Rasta Rabbit gently took Layla from his pocket.

He explained "Layla, future queen of Rastaland, heiress to King Solomon's throne, Welcome home! We have made it successfully through the Witches Woods, escaped the alligator regulators and made it to Truth's Tower. Inside resides your father Osiris, the chief, king and leader of Rastaland. His queen, your mother Isis of sun, fire and earth. They will further explain your place, the reason you've come and what must be done in the kingdom."

Rasta Rabbit began clapping his hand like paws, instantly Layla began to grow taller. Rasta Rabbit stopped clapping his hands but Layla continued to grow! Over the trees, she moved her head from side to side receiving a glimpse of the buildings and some towers, taking in Rastaland, the beings, greenery and odd birds, then she begin to shrink until she was a little shorter than Rasta Rabbit.

"Habari Gani Queen, shall we?", grunted Rasta Rabbit with a laugh handing her a purple dress the same color as the jumper she wore when she entered Rastaland and some open toe sandals with flats that matched the dress perfectly. He turned his back to her as she got dressed, the clothes fitting superbly. Once she finished Rasta Rabbit took her by the arm and they proceeded towards the Tower of Truth.

Layla gazed up at the castle that stood enormous and welcoming before her. There were carvings and statues, beautiful gardens and flowers surrounding the configuration.

As Layla and Rasta Rabbit approached the gate, she admired the masks inscribed on the Tower before seeing lions that barricaded the entry!

"Jambo!" greeted Rasta Rabbit.

"Hoi, en hoe gaat het Hoot?!" (*Hi, and how are you Hoot?*), said the talking Lion.

"Goed! Ik ga naar Layla's Labyrinth" (*Great! I'm going to Layla's Labyrinth*) replied Rasta Rabbit.

"Hoi empress" (*Hi*) nodded the talking Lion, now turning his attention to Layla.

Layla looked into his golden eyes he was a blond lion with golden locks. Everything she had ever considered normal had flown out of her mind the moment she was sucked into the weed stalk. Now she had to answer a talking lion!

"Jambo!" said Layla, the new greeting spilling from her lips naturally.

"We hebben je zo gemist! (*We have missed you so!*) Welcome back Empress!", with this the lion opened the gate and Layla followed closely behind the Rabbit. The scent of 'Kush' and 'Frankincense' enticed her nostrils, she felt really warm and her ears began to tingle.

She saw birds and angels in the sky they both had red, gold and green wings. The village was busy with beings running in and out of multicolored buildings that had signs in a language Layla didn't comprehend. The being's faces were alien to anything her mind could conceive. Some had no eye lids, or one big eye in the middle of their head, in colors she couldn't define, red and brown mixed with an illusion that was now her reality.

Variant species ambled about her in a world all their own! Others resembled animals from earth with human limbs. Dressed in bright colors, Layla noticed that both the men and women had long dreadlocks. Some had antennas, while others had tails. Children hopped around her and what seemed like giant birds hovered above her, but when Layla looked closer she saw that they were actually devices the beings were travelling in.

Rasta Rabbit lead the way to a café, the dwelling fluctuated above a body of water. Grabbing her hand, Rasta Rabbit guided her over the bridge towards the entrance.

The billboard above the door read 'Rasta Baby'. Layla smiled inwardly to herself, despite her nerves, the name of the café made her feel welcome. The outside of the café was red, the inside décor was green and black. A black floor with seven sets of green chairs and tables filled the room. There was a bar and customers in the far right of the café. A few citizens relaxed at the tables, conversing with one another, while others read documents that floated above their heads. Reggae music played low and mellow from a source Layla could not see.

Rasta Rabbit greeted many patrons there before ushering Layla to a table near the back of the coffee bar. Layla loved the art work in the establishment. The wall was one big piece of ingenuity! The red walls were covered with piercing illustrations. The beings of Rastaland on a great day, worshipping life, was the story it told. A mural was attached to the partition near the bar. It was of a Rasta man, floor length dreadlocks and bread, with wings that opened filling the entire back drop of the painting. The vibrant colors of gold, blue, green and orange filled the sketches and flowed into the atmosphere. As the smell of ganja pervaded the air, Layla observed patrons blowing out smoke that danced mid-air before evaporating.

Pulling out her chair, a true gentleman, he waited until she was comfortable before taking a seat across from her.

"Before we enter your labyrinth, I wanted to explain a little bit about what you're observing." Rasta Rabbit began with a smile.

"Okay" breathed Layla.

Rasta Rabbit could see from her big watery eyes that she was all ears, curious to learn about his dimension and petrified all at once!

"Tell me what you know about the solar system?" inquired Rasta Rabbit.

"I know there are eight planets now since they dropped Pluto, It used to be nine." answered Layla.

"Pluto still exists, as does Rastaland, Pluto is a star, Rastaland is a realm," explained Rasta Rabbit.

"Realm?" Layla questioned.

"A royal domain or empire within anything occurs, prevails or dominates; the realm of dreams, explained best by dictionary.com on your planet," spoke Rasta Rabbit in a robotic voice.

"Realm?" Layla asked again, right eyebrow arched.

"Name the planets," asked Rasta Rabbit, "In order," he concluded.

"You can't answer a question with a question," grunted Layla.

"Jambo! iedereen, wil je iets drinken?", (*Hello everyone, would you like something to drink*), interrupted the waiter.

Dressed in a red pants suit and turban, to Layla his face was a coalescence of a bear and alien. He had the longest feet Layla had saw on a being, encased in red boots. His bear arms held his tray atop his protruding belly.

"Hoi Bakvet, we zullen moeten twee waters, alsjeblieft", (*Hi Bakvet, we shall have two waters, please*), spoke Rasta Rabbit, answering the monster and ordering drinks it sounded like to Layla.

"Goed, zal ik het raam open doen?", (*Good, shall I open the window?*), spoke the waiter.

"Ja, dank je", (*Yes, thank you*), answered Rasta Rabbit.

"Jambo! Princesa," greeted the waiter, his eyes on Layla as he reached around her opening the window to her left.

Layla sat frozen, staring into the transparent eyes of this being. No pupils, his eyes were two yellow balls, but Layla knew he could see her. Dreadfully she turned to Rasta Rabbit for help!

"Don't be rude Princesa, speak sistah!" was his response.

"Hi" grunted Layla, the 'H' a moan and the 'I' catching in her throat, she didn't think he heard her, but gratefully he spread his red lips and smiled, exposing his gold grill, before retreating to the bar.

"I know you're apprehensive but never be afraid to speak. Rather it's your mind or a greeting." scolded Rasta Rabbit.

"Being nice is the last thing on my mind right now!" spoke Layla raising her voice, causing some of the patrons to turn in their direction.

"So snarky! Where were we?" replied Rasta Rabbit.

"Realm!" repeated Layla.

"Name the planets in the order you were instructed in school. I will then explain where the realm of Rastaland resides in relation to them" Rasta Rabbit.

Layla gazed at Rasta Rabbit for a few seconds, fighting the anxiety that rose like bile in her throat. She felt as if she was at home when her computer was slow and she was trying to get something done! Or like the many times the universe was taking to long to deliver...her way! She wanted answers now! And she didn't feel revisiting school sessions past would grant them!

"Uw drankjes", (*Your drinks*), spoke Bakvet as he sat drinks down on the table.

Layla let out an exasperated breath, looking in the direction of the receding waiter. By the time she turned to face Rasta Rabbit she had regained her composure.

"There is the Sun, Mercury, Venus, Earth, Mars, Jupiter, Saturn, Uranus, and Neptune and like I said there *was* Pluto."

"You're not a dummy after all!" smiled Rasta Rabbit.

"Now answer my question." demanded Layla.

"Between each planet you named there are portals that lead to other dimensions, planets, stars and realms. The Rastaland realm is located between Jupiter and Saturn; the seventh realm from the Sun and planet Earth. There are infinite dimensions and portals as there are stars in the sky, more even, our creator is as limitless as space is." Rasta Rabbit explained.

Layla took a moment to sip the clear blue liquid the waiter had placed in front of her. It tasted like grape Kool-Aid, cold and sugary to perfection.

"How do you know about dictionary.com?" asked Layla, flashing back to his definition of realm.

"When I was sent to Earth to retrieve you, I tapped into your different forms of research. Humans are fascinating beings! I was proud and blessed to discover your parent's, Osiris and Isis are still greatly respected throughout the land and even worshipped in parts of Egypt. But whoa! I'm getting ahead of myself! I want to elaborate more about where you are, then you'll understand more about who you are and why you're here" concluded Rasta Rabbit.

"Please" Layla.

"Your father will explain with visual details soon, but for now I'll give a semi-brief summary." begin Rasta Rabbit "Ras Fela is the patriarch of Rastaland, lover of the creator of life,

life itself. This is his Eden! The beings you behold are as different yet similar as the human beings are on Earth. You have various ethnicities but your all the same, though you speak different dialects, have variant skin, eye and hair color, you all bleed, cry, were born and will die. Our subsistence parallel in that aspect, yet we are higher evolved beings here, who marry each others soul and read one another's minds.

Our native tongue is LaRoz, a composition of dialects from other realms, dimensions, planets and beings. The vocabulary that we exercise from Earth was chosen after your departure from Rastaland, picked up from travelling to and from Earth trying to break Winter's spell over you. For example the Dutch we speak, Ras Fela chose from your life together in Holland. The Swahili we speak is Osiris's choice for your short time together in Dar Es Salaam Tanzania. The Spanish we speak is Isis's choice for her love of Che Guevara and your collective time in Cuba. We can visit those lives later in this journey if you like?" asked Rasta Rabbit.

"Sure", croaked Layla sipping more of her drink to ease her scratchy throat and thoughts. She felt as if she was playing make believe, her first mushroom trip relived!

"Why that face?" asked Rasta Rabbit smiling at her expression.

"Just remembering my first mushroom trip," truthfully answered Layla "I feel like I did then, crazy!"

"Well we could visit that memory too if you like." grinned Rasta Rabbit.

"No! It was a roller coaster ride that lasted eight hours! No thanks. Please continue" Layla.

"Okay, there are many beings in Rastaland, let's begin with the spirits you see around you." Rasta Rabbit began "The bartender Bakvet is a war-wah-zi being." Rasta Rabbit pronounced each syllable slowly before continuing. "The warwahzi are servants here in Rastaland, they speak all languages according to their house hold. Most are bartenders, butlers, maids, etc."

Rasta Rabbit paused as Layla took in the warwahzi creature attending customers. He was big and tall, the top of his bald head grazing the ceiling. His skin was the color of red dirt, he had antennas on each side of his head, no ears and his yellow eyes bulged out of his face. His red hands had six fingers on each hand and he worked studiously, caring for each client. Turning her attention back to Rasta Rabbit, Layla smiled before speaking.

"He's handsome" she grimaced.

"Take care not to shun all you consider alien." stated Rasta Rabbit at Layla's reaction.

"He's alien alright!" grunted Layla slightly.

"You're just as foreign to him as he is to you" informed Rasta Rabbit.

"True" observed Layla.

"Never judge," stated Rasta Rabbit "Now, most here among us are sun, moon and star entities in physical form. Your mother is a sun being and you will soon see her in bodily mould. We can take on any physical shape we choose, but unless you're a shape shifter as your father or half shape shifter like me, you cannot change forms once the Most High and your soul has created who you will become. The same as Earth, you live and die as a human, never altering from a man into a lion as some with shape shifter blood can here. Yet if you are a sun or star being you can always revert back to that state.

We also have angels, forest and lake creatures, humanoid panthers, lions and tigers. There are air entities that float about and can be seen dancing when the universe's sweet ganja is blown into the aerosphere." Rasta Rabbit said staring out the window at the floating air beings that passed.

"So those afloat are sun, moon and star beings?" Layla asked.

"Some are, others are birds of Rastaland, some shape shifters, others elevated beings." answered Rasta Rabbit.

"And I'm half shape shifter?" Layla asked.

"Yes and half fire!" answered Rasta Rabbit.

"Can you explain more about the beings of this realm?" Layla requested.

"Certainly, the sun clan speaks our native tongue LaRoz, exist on the sun, their and your power is light. The star clan speak LaRoz, live in heavens vault, their powers are light and fire, cousin to the sun and moon. Now the humanoid Lions are guards for your father, most form his army the Rasta Renegades, they speak LaRoz, Spanish and Dutch, their powers being their wisdom and strength to name a few. Humanoid Panthers guard Ras Fela, reside in Fela's Forest and are shape shifter, speaking all languages of Rastaland. There are numerous creatures here, but most significantly the Alligator Regulators are the ones to watch, among others. The Regulators that protect your father are embellished with Rasta colored armor, the Witches Regulators armor is white and can be clearly identified by the glistening ice. You will learn the difference, your survival depends on it!" explained Rasta Rabbit, leaning back in his chair, he sighed, taking a breath before he continued.

"This is our seventh and final attempt to break the spell Winter placed on you. The eighth time would have cancelled out any other tries. Winter committed a cowardly betrayal that earns her the execration of all who remain loyal to her cause. She has caused so much pain and intends to inflict more! Yet we will pray and fight her with love! You will come to know and love all these beautiful beings Winter yearns to destroy! She wants mind control! Total control! On Earth you have commercials and stereotypes, things you strive to accomplish, you compete, you kill and love. Winter covets our powers, our faith the elements that makes us who we are! She has taken you from all that you have known! Placed you within reach, but so far away, your aunt Cleo is seer of Earth, yet she could not break the binding curse Winter held upon you! We had our greatest wizard create a potion that would get me and you back here. I had to go through different portals to discover the correct route to get to where you were on Earth. Once we had the potion and portals and you were here, I had to smuggle you deeper into Rastaland, we came in through Pallid, our city located in Ivory Heights; Winter's territory. I couldn't trust that you could move with your mind upon arrival, I felt slipping you in would be uncomplicated." Rasta Rabbit.

"You didn't explain how you got me here?" inquired Layla.

"The weed stalk doll! Its similar to your labyrinth we are going to." Rasta Rabbit.

"My labyrinth?" Layla asked.

"Yes you have a labyrinth, a city and a kingdom here Princesa, this is your home. Now let's hit this spliff and drift to the labyrinth!" winked Rasta Rabbit grabbing a spliff from the pile on the table, lighting it.

"So all these, what I assumed were decorative flowers on the table are rolled joints?" laughed Layla.

"Flowers indeed! Flowers indeed!" Rasta Rabbit smiled blowing out smoke. "Smoke up!" Rasta Rabbit said offering Layla the joint.

She inhaled pure bliss and exhaled some of the most

flawless ganja her lungs had ever tasted. She felt a slight tingle on her third pull. The potent smoke making her hazy reality a three dimension, dimension!

"Let's go before we can't" said Rasta Rabbit standing.

Layla tilted forward a bit, catching herself by grabbing the table. She smiled her embarrassment away before taking Rasta Rabbits waiting hand.

***

The Rastaland sun blew her buzz a bit, the bizarre creatures bringing her back to the moment. Meandering behind Rasta Rabbit, Layla smiled at the abstract individuals, Rasta Rabbit laughed as Layla ducked, thinking she would be hit by a soaring wing, dodging their everyday traffic.

Now deeper within the city that resided behind the tower walls, Layla viewed a taller column, discrepant from the rest. Gold with red and green carvings, beings flew in and out of the windows, Layla saw no other entry.

As they got closer she noticed the ground was covered in drawings as were all the surrounding buildings she saw. The dirt was red and around the big beautiful green bushes, Rasta colored tulips were planted dancing in the wind. Layla held tight to Rabbits jacket as he whizzed towards the tower. They walked for awhile before reaching a wall covered in vines. The Rabbit turned to Layla and spit a rhyme "Will you please touch a vine/so that your labyrinth will unwind"

Layla moved towards the vine with caution, looking into the eyes of the Rabbit the entire time. She stretched her arm and touched a vine. The wall separated and the Rabbit pulled Layla through the open center.

They arrived in a passage way, everything was covered in vines, the walls, ground and doors that aligned the long corridor. It was a peaceful place no sound could be heard besides what sounded like flapping wings inside the walls. The Rabbit squeezed Layla's hand.

"Dada, this labyrinth was designed for your return. It's the tunnel to your past, similar to the weed stalk in the forest. I am honored to be your escort. We shall proceed to Majesty Hall where your parents await your arrival. I know that this is overwhelming and new to your line of thinking. But keep an open mind and allow your heart to lead you! Again my sweet, welcome home!" He pulled Layla down the exquisite entrance way. Her eyes drinking in the moving vines and artifacts that aligned the walls, her heart alert, her mind somewhere between yesterday and now, her legs strong, leading her to her purpose, her life's destination. Squeezing the Rabbits fingers she braced herself for what was to come!

CHAPTER THREE LAYLA'S LABYRINTH

Layla and Rasta Rabbit walked towards the back of the labyrinth, Rasta Rabbit lead her to a vine covered wall; that opened as their entrance into a garden.

Layla squinted against the glaring sun that raided her eye sockets upon entering the allotment. She immediately heard "She's not the right Layla" being whispered by the small mice, cats, dogs and indescribable insects that scurried along the path. The animals, beings and atmosphere charged with an energy that was electric, Layla felt faint and nervous, her palms sweating and her heart was beating fast.

She gripped the Rabbits hand and her once resilient stance began to falter. They walked along a path made of multicolored rocks. The labyrinth was full of greenery, flowers and trees. The exquisite fortress was as tall as the eye could see. Its multicolored tiles shifting colors and position as a red, gold, green and black flag flapped in the warm breeze.

Layla noticed that the air was a steady warm breeze blowing the cherry smelling air around. Birds and beings floated in the air, along with what appeared to be angels with red, gold and green wings and halos. The Rasta colored flowers were singing some African song and Layla heard drums being played in the distance. Layla felt as if she was dreaming, she was just about to ask Rasta Rabbit to pinch her when a humanoid fox female interrupted their path.

Her upper half was fox; fox face and ears, red, gold and green bows, one on each ear. She had on a red, gold and green tutu and boots. She blew on a gold bull horn before screaming

"Welkom Princesa Layla, we hebben gewacht voor u", (*Welcome Princess Layla, we have been waiting for you*), greets the Fox Lady.

"She speaks English" informs Rasta Rabbit.

"Te hemos estado esperando", (*We have been waiting for you*), greets the Fox Lady once more.

"English," repeats Rasta Rabbit.

"Welcome Princess Layla, we have been awaiting your arrival! My name is Ras Fox and I'll be your escort to the king," Ras Fox replied, shaking her head from side to side, as if to call the English language forth before blowing her horn once more. The half human, half lizard guards that were on either side of Ras Fox looked like the same lizard guards that stopped them before also patrolled the portal. Upon hearing Ras Fox bull horn they stepped aside.

"Are those the same lizard men that we came across when we first entered Rastaland?" a puzzled Layla questioned Rasta Rabbit.

"No, there are many alligator regulators used as soldiers and guards. Some are good and some work for the White Witch," Rasta Rabbit explained.

"Is this a dream?" Layla asked.

"Shall we?" Rasta Rabbit replied pulling her along, through the gate regulators, following close behind Ras Fox.

The passage opened up before them as they tread on the heels of Ras Fox and the regulators. The ground glowed with each of their steps. Red, gold and green lights lit up beneath their footsteps. It reminded Layla of Michael Jackson's 'Billie Jean' video.

The entrance hall looked like a dark tunnel, becoming illuminated with each step. The walls were engraved with illustrations that chroniclized Rastaland's inception. Abruptly Ras Fox ceased walking, continuing a few steps ahead the Alligator Regulators stopped as well. Ras Fox blew her trumpet, a fog immediately enveloped them. When the mist lifted Layla stood alone in the vestibule. A crowd assembled on each side of her, the beings, some half human, others animals she never saw before, dressed in garments that sparkled. The sparkles gave the hall a magical feel. The path before her lead to the King and Queen of Rastaland who were seated on a golden platform, the gold and silver base of their throne stemmed upward like a flower, the petals forming seats for the royal members.

"Welkom Princesa Layla" greeted the king standing. The beings all stood and bowed in unison.

Layla noticed Rasta Rabbit was bowing near the throne. The king was a tall man of Carmel complexion. His locks touching the floor, his beard as well, his golden crown glistened and the gold chain he wore had a red, gold and green charm that rotated around its axis. The queen was regal in her stance, dark skin and slender royalty reeking from her essence.

Layla begin to walk towards the throne, passing the bowing citizens. She reached the king and shook his out stretched hand.

"Your Royal Highness" Layla.

"Father or Papa would be more appropriate. Welkom thuis dochter" said the King.

"Thuis?" repeated Layla.

"Home, Welcome home my Rasta baby!" said the King.

"Am I dreaming?" asked Layla.

"No, you are remembering my love, you have not been

home for awhile and there is a lot I must tell you. I know that everything must seem extreme. Yet keep an open mind here in our dimension, your dimension Princesa. Now Ras Fox has brought you a seat", continued the King.

Layla turned to see a golden chair behind her she sat as the King continued speaking. "And I will now take the time to elucidate and create an understanding. Princesa, it is time for you to uphold your rightful position. The evil of our world is threatening to rise up and spill over into our amicable utopia. Layla, we have brought you back from the brink of annihilation. You are our greatest weapon in conquering the White Witch Winter who jeopardizes Rastaland's very existence! But before you can assume your role in defeating the White Witch, you must conceive the unconceivable, open your mind to the unknown, throw away all that you ever learned on earth! Only then will you have the ability to know who you are, where you come from and why you are back. You have the sovereignty to prevail, you hold the sleutels Princesa!"

***

CHAPTER FOUR: OSIRIS SPEAKS

Layla became stoic in the golden chair that was put aside for her, by Ras Fox and continued to listen to the King of Rastaland speak.

"I am your father Layla, my name is Osiris, and this is your mother, empress of Rastaland the Isis of fire. You were sent away by your aunt White Witch Winter. We have been searching for your soul for centuries. We have searched earth and other planets, interrogated beings in other dimensions. The curse that she placed on your vital force can only be broken when you kill her, breaking the binding spell, she will have to take your life on Earth so that we may capture your soul in that moment, earth because that's where Winter binded you with her anathema, we shall collect your soul there and guide you home where you shall remain and reign forever! The White Witch has also deleted your memory, however she will never expunge the love we have for you Princesa! Your position is immortal! Now before you and our citizens, council, guards and servants, I shall reveal Rastaland's history"

Layla along with the rest of the audience watched as a large screen was lowered behind the throne. Layla also noticed an empty golden pew in between the King and Queen's, she felt in her soul that that seat belonged to her!

As King Osiris spoke, images that reflected his words and complimented his narration shown on the transmitter.

"Ras Fela is the founder of Rastaland. He resided on the star Pluto and planet earth to name a few. He was a master in every life!"

As King Osiris described Ras Fela he appeared on the screen, a handsome man, midnight skin regal posture.

"When Ras Fela returned to God after completing his mission on planet Pluto, he asked God if he could have authority over God's star Rastadormis. Rastadormis was unoccupied celestial amplitude. God granted Ras Fela dominion over Rastadormis, he renamed the star Rastaland. Rastaland is a place of peace, many beings dwell here from every area in the universe." stated Osiris.

He continued, "For Thee Creator not only created heaven and earth, but many dimensions, planets and higher evolved beings. Once a soul has gone to our maker he can decide if it wants to stay in Thee Creator's embrace or complete another soul mission. Many beings have come to Rastaland to rebuild, explore and preserve conciliation. Though our sphere is titled Rastaland and Rastafarism is a religion on your planet, we all know that there is only *one* God which makes us all *one*! Praising God is our main objective, loving God and knowing that God is the creator of all things, the Most High being the reason I am, I was, I be, you are welkom hier!"

Layla observed the crowd in unison bowing on their knees chanting 'All praise, exalt, honor and respect to the Most High, Lord of Lord, King of Kings, God of all things and beings, Selah'

After their salute to the Most High the spectators took their seats and focused once again on the King who continued his narration.

"So though our dimension is titled Rastaland, we welkom open minds from all realms, and as it was on your planet Layla, planet earth, here we must also persevere against the hostilities that terrorize our very spirits. The invasion of the White Witch

Winter has been our greatest calamity!"

A picture of the White Witch Winter ran across the screen causing the audience to gasp. She had platinum locks, albino skin, red eyes, blue lips and long nails that curved upward. King Osiris continued.

"Here in Rastaland we have powers that we hold dear as the Most High gifts! We have the ability to fly, we are element benders and shape shifters. Because we are such a puissant realm, the Witch covets to abduct our powers of retention. She is attempting to obliterate our memories! If she succeeds she will be capable of ruining Rastaland. We brought you here to train you in things you already know by heart, here you must re-remember! You must destroy the White Witch before the seventh full moon, which will be your twenty first birthday. At twenty-one your powers will reach a height that surpasses mine and your mother's. You will have the grace of God and the will power of your ancestors, if the Witch had kept you hidden after your twenty first birthday, we would have no chance in defeating her. Now that we have you here, we must move fast, you will have three soul missions to complete by the seventh full moon; first discovering the Witches weakness, second you must be prepared to defeat Winter after we subdue her army, and finally you must melt her heart that is kept inside Ice Mountain. You will learn more about our realm and your prestige in the coming moons; I could never tell or show all that you need to know in one setting. Yet, welkom home Princesa, Rasta Rabbit Hoot will be your guide, you shall meet Ras Fela, he has been waiting a long time to see you again. You will be educated by the best and you will defeat the White Witch Winter!"

CHAPTER FIVE: RASTA STATE OF MIND

Layla blinked and was back in the labyrinth she entered before her session with the king. She turned to her right and discovered Rasta Rabbit having a conversation with a red tulip.

"How did we get back here?" she inquired causing Rasta Rabbit to jump out of his conversation literally.

"Here in Rastaland we move with our minds, you should try it!" Rasta Rabbit replied.

"What do you mean, *move with our minds*?" asked Layla.

"Think of a place mentally and transport yourself there physically with your brain waves. Somatically explore your introspections." explained Rasta Rabbit.

Layla thought back to where she was before this all began. Closing her eyes, once more she felt the climate around her converting the pressure of time and memories into reality.

Layla and Rasta Rabbit had returned to the forest, standing by the stalk that sucked her in.

"How did we get back here? Back to this forest, back to earth?" inquired Layla.

"You thought us here!" responded Rasta Rabbit.

"This is the stalk that sucked me into Rastaland! Gosh, life seemed much simpler before that occurred!" fussed Layla.

"This mission that is life, this venture, this present that is a gift, our voyage, journey, we must love every element of it of us! One moment defines us the next destroys, and your brain inside your head, your imagination, the chemical imbalances in your mind that makes what you see make sense in your world. Well, your mind is the pivotal source in your world and ours! But unlike beings on your planet, we don't second guess ourselves, nor force ourselves to adapt to ephemeral environments. We do more than say we will change, we 'think it' into existence!" Rasta Rabbit.

"So we can go anywhere I think up?" questioned Layla.

"Let's begin with visiting your past, once you've mastered implementing mind control, your future feats will be effortless, that said let's begin our game of mind and seek!" Rasta Rabbit.

Layla thought back to one of her happiest moments, receiving her BMW Z6, she knew it was a materialistic moment but it held great visual affect in her memory.

"Surprise, yelled her family and friends."

Layla opened her eyes in the midst of her nineteenth birthday celebration. Everyone was there as they had been before, smiling and inviting. Nothing had changed in this year old memory, she heard her father's voice and knew what was coming next, could she end this memory before her drunken uncle arrives and begins the soul train line, ignoring him she turned her attention to the exquisite piece of machinery, topped with a red bow in the driveway!

"Do you like your car?" Layla's mother asked her, her face so close Layla could smell cake icing on her breath.

"It's what I've always wanted" Layla responded.

Looking deep into her mother's eyes, Layla exhaled in the

moment, reaching her hand out to touch her car; she realized it was Rasta Rabbits shoulder.

"Hey! You're not my brand new BMW before I dented the fender a month later!" shouted Layla pulling her hand back and realizing they were still in the forest in the same instant.

"I am not! Just your guide through this energy maze" laughed Rasta Rabbit spreading his arms apart and twirling around.

"How can you visit a moment that's already passed?" Layla asked.

"Because everything happens simultaneously in time, so where on earth and in Rastaland, you've already defeated the White Witch! Yet physically you have to catch up to your future moments and your future moments can always change if you choose a different path in that point in time" explained Rasta Rabbit.

"What? Can you alter the past?" asked Layla.

"You know as a human you utilize a certain percentage of your brain; I'm going to need you to tap into that other percent if you're to ever understand your mission. I told King Osiris we should have captured and trained you as a young soul. Adults are so hard to convert! You have to constantly repeat yourself, they NEVER believe what they hear or see the first thousand times around!" Rasta Rabbit shouted working himself up.

"My mind is open; you must be patient Rabbit!" Layla said being pulled into his frustration.

"No, you can't change the past you can relive it for a few seconds. Yet once you've acquired the technique, in the future you can jump into an old memory for a few seconds of protection. Or you can transform a moment you're in by thinking your way out of it. For example, if you're confronted by the White Witch and her army, you can dive into your favorite memory about your car to escape, or you could think labyrinth and return there physically using your mind. The labyrinth is your safe haven; think of the labyrinth any time you feel threaten." Informed Rasta Rabbit.

"Ok, so you can't change the past, just visit and you can change the future…" Layla.

"No, you can't change the future, you choose who you are and what you want to be in every moment, so the future is always changing." Interrupted Rasta Rabbit.

"What?" Layla.

"At your party for instance, you could have wanted another car, or changed the way you felt about the car, the people at the party, anything! We are always evolving changing our minds, choosing something different, so whatever plans you have for the future can always change.

But if you're ever in danger, for example in a fire in the future, all you would have to do is think rain and put the fire out!" Rasta Rabbit explained.

"So you can think something and it will happen?" Layla.

"Yes, this is not such a foreign idea! You can do the same thing on earth! You think of someone and they call. You feel like something intense is about to happen and it does. You project with your mind your entire life. However, as a human, you've allowed fear and stress to keep you from immediate results. Yet as the Princesa of Rastaland you have the ability to free your mind of its imbedded restraints and explore your thoughts mentally and physically.

"And we will begin by revisiting your past lives as promised in the café. In doing so, maybe you will be less confused about time travel and your mission as future Queen of Rastaland. I shall divide this travel session into two sections. The first you can relax, relate and review. The second you can follow me with another game we call mind and seek or memory seek. The introductory is a walk in the park for you, but you will put some work in later. All you have to do to begin friend is take my hand" smiled Rasta Rabbit tipping his hat with his left, digging in his pocket afterwards pulling out a joint and begin smoking as he extending his right hand to Layla.

Layla was enveloped within a cloud of weed smoke the moment their skin made contact. Holding onto Rasta Rabbit's hand she found herself behind Osiris, Isis, Ras Fela and her aunt Cleo in deep conversation.

Turning to Rasta Rabbit their eyes connected, before Layla could part her lips, Rasta Rabbit began to explain.

"We are in Amsterdam, Holland the year is 1777, wrap up of the Golden Age for this country. Ships have sailed from all over the world, from the Baltic Sea to Brazil forming the basis of a worldwide trading network. Yet the wars in the eighteenth and nineteenth centuries between the Dutch Republic, England and France shall take its toll on sweet Amsterdam. Now all is well and this is the year and place of your first citing on Earth under Winter's curse. Your aunt Cleo, the spectacular sister to your far right, next to your mother, has just found you! Cleo…"

"They can't hear us?" asked Layla interrupting Rasta Rabbit.

Taking in the décor, a museum filled with Dutch and African artifacts. The floors, walls and ceilings were covered in Egyptian hieroglyphics. The atmosphere took her breath away and seven feet away from her, four people stood in a huddle.

"Ras Fela may be sensitive enough to pick up a vibration from our entering this moment, but not the others and Ras Fela will know that this visit is for instructional purposes, ova standing our presence here." Rasta Rabbit related.

"Is Ras Fela, Horus, son of Osiris and Isis?" Layla inquired

"Yes! How precise and astute of you!" smirked Rasta Rabbit.

"So, Ras Fela is my brother?" questioned Layla.

"Yes and you shall create a history as grand as your family's legacy in Rastaland" answered Rasta Rabbit.

"In some myths Horus parents were Nut and Geb" Layla.

"And as you've implied they were myths" Rasta Rabbit.

"On Earth this entire scenario would be a myth!" noted Layla.

"Well, as written by Greek historian Diodorus Siculus, who wrote about North Africa, declaring that Ausar or Osiris was a real king, credited with founding Kemet (Egypt) and India. Ausar's, your father, tomb was found under the Gaza plateau very close to the Sphinx" explained Rasta Rabbit.

"Wow" Layla exclaimed "You're the smart one!"

"Just well informed" Rasta Rabbit.

"So, what are they discussing?" Layla asked.

"You" answered Rasta Rabbit.

"What about me? And how can Ras Fela, Osiris, Isis and Cleo look exactly as they do in 2010 as they did in 1777?" asked Layla.

"We are timeless! And that is not how they look in 1777." said Rasta Rabbit hitting the joint and blowing out more smoke.

They were back in the labyrinth.

"Oops" giggled Rasta Rabbit, blowing out more smoke and they were in the same place but now the groups huddled in front of them were white!

"Where did they go?" inquired Layla.

"That's them; in 1777 they came to Earth to search for you

when they found out which continent, country and city, they had to mimic the environment. They most certainly couldn't be African and roam the country *freely* in 1777 Europe. There standing in the same place, your father is the tall man, hold on let's split the scenery, hold me tight, we must keep close contact at all times during these past life ventures or you'll be back in labyrinth and I'd be here talking to myself, I keep you in the moment, so to speak!" Rasta Rabbit.

Layla never lost contact as she let go of his hand, easing her had up his arm, tightening her grip on his upper arm.

Rasta Rabbit hit his joint as he exhaled he split the smoke in half with his hand.

Layla could then see the room in front of her divided in half. Same scenery, the scene on the right held the black circle of people the scene on her left held the white circle.

"The black Osiris, Isis, Ras Fela and Cleo on the right are the same as the white Osiris, Isis, Ras Fela and Cleo on the left. In segregating the energy, you have the opportunity to glimpse the magic of their disguise." said Rasta Rabbit.

"Your parents, brother and aunt set out on a mission to find you. Cleo revealed Winter had sent you to Earth, this narrowed down the search tremendously, we new from the start we had a limited time to find you and bring you home.

Cleo spotted you in Amsterdam, one of her favorite places on Earth. Let's focus our attention on the left circle, you're about to enter the gallery." wrapped up Rasta Rabbit.

Turning their attention to the left, Layla smiled as a Dutch woman holding the hand of a small girl entered the room. The woman wore a purple bonnet and white sack-back gown. The child was beautifully dressed in a pink bonnet, booties, socks and waist coat. Her white dress was trimmed in lace coming to her knees.

"How do they know that's me?" asked Layla.

"Just watch." winked Rasta Rabbit.

When the little girl noticed Osiris, Isis, Ras Fela and Cleo she ran to them.

***

"Mama! Papa!" she screamed jumping into Isis arms.

"Mama, Tante Winter is heir! Mijn geheugen is vervagen! Ze probeert te wissen me!", (Mama, aunt Winter is here! My memory is fading! She is trying to erase me), past Layla said, continuing to hug Isis tightly around her neck.

Her Earth mother stood back in awe, Isis held her tight.

***

"As a seven-year-old child in the beginning of the curse you retained your memory, you were smart enough to know what your aunt had done and knew your time was limited and your powers of retention were fading." Rasta Rabbit inserted observing Layla engrossed in the scene that played out before her.

***

"We moeten nu vertrekken! (We must leave now!)" Isis stated facing Osiris clutching little Layla to her chest.

"The portal pressures would crush her; we could kill her in the process" answered Ras Fela.

"Rieker windmill!" spoke Osiris.

***

Layla was no longer in the museum, now she was in an open space surrounded by trees, a river and pedestrians.

"Are we in Vondel Park now?" present Layla asked Rasta Rabbit, expressing her knowledge of Holland.

"No, Vondel Park wasn't established in Amsterdam until 1864. Were at Rieker windmill, Rembrandt used to walk along this river and create landscape drawings. In time this area will become Amstel Park." answered Rasta Rabbit, the windmill stood proud and powerful along the Amstel River.

"It's one of eight windmills here in Holland" smiled Rasta Rabbit glancing at Layla taken in De Rieker windmill.

"Your family has gathered here to convene and assist you while you still remember." interrupted Rasta Rabbit.

They turned their attention to her family assembled by the windmill. When Isis put little Layla down, she began to speak.

***

"Mijn familie es goed, maar velen stierven in de plaag", (My family is good, but many died in the plague), said Little Layla.

"Winter..." little Layla began before bursting into tears, Isis picked her up again as the others concocted a game plan.

"Waar is zij nu?", (Where is she now?), asked Ras Fela.

"Hoi broer! Hoi! (Hi brother! Hi!)", exclaimed Little Layla leaping from Isis arms into Ras Fela's.

"Ik weet niet waar Winter is. (I don't know where Winter is)", answered Little Layla.

***

"So" spoke Rasta Rabbit breaking into Layla's line of vision, she had been totally engrossed in Isis and Little Layla's interaction.

"They will discover that they cannot take you with them without breaking the curse. Also, they must leave before Winter knows anything. If she detects their presence here she would send you to another planet or dimension, starting their search all over again. You shared this day with them, a day you kept in your heart until your life ended here and you resurfaced forty-six years later in Tanzania, Africa. Ras Fela stayed behind as your guardian in this life. Disguised as a Dutch man, he guided and protected your every move. He was a great brother and you loved him for abiding by you. I'll give you a glimpse of that in this next review." Rasta Rabbit expounded.

Rasta Rabbit took out his joint, hit it and blew out smoke, the thick cloud covered everything and Layla could no longer see her family by the windmill. When the smoke cleared, she felt high and the scenery had changed. Rasta Rabbit begin to explain.

"You lived enough seasons to observe the space that held De Rieker windmill become Amstel Park. The year is 1850, the year of your death in this life. Ras Fela and you are in tuned to this transition, you've met here to discuss it. You're seventy-seven years old." Rasta Rabbit concluded.

Layla smiled as she viewed the older version of herself ambling down a familiar path to meet her beloved brother.

Dressed in a white gown with a colorful bonnet atop her head, she looked well for an older woman, her smile lit up the sky when her eyes drank in Ras Fela's approach.

Long silver hair, sporting a black top hat and trench coat, Ras Fela looked distinguished as always.

The two embraced before sitting on a bench and starting their conversation.

***

"Hoe heeft de tijd is die u behandelen broer? (How has time been treating brother?)", *Old Layla began.*

"Goed! (Good!)", *said Ras Fela.*

Old Layla stared off into space for awhile, grabbing her brother's hand to hold before she began.

"Ik ben ziek (I am sick)", *speaking the words into her brother's eyes, Old Layla began to cry.*

"Wat zal worden mijn aarde familie zodra ik weg ben? (What will become of my Earth family once I'm gone?)" Old Layla asked, getting straight to the point of their meeting.

Ras Fela leaned his full back against the bench, he gazed long and hard at his sister, knowing he would not see her for centuries after this conversation.

***

"Here comes the hard part" whispered Rasta Rabbit to Present Layla, he had been her translator and now he squeezed her arm tighter bracing for what he knew was next.

***

"Jouw familie komt wel goed, zult u altijd worden aangesloten. (Your family will be fine; you will always be connected)" Ras Fela began breaking into the silence. He

grabbed his sister's face and kissed each cheek.

"Maar het is 1850 en misschien niet meer terug te komen Rastaland tot 2010! (But it is 1850 and you might not come back to Rastaland until 2010!)", Ras Fela shed this news nervously, bowing his head in sadness.

"Dat lang? (That long?)", screamed Old Layla.

"Ja (Yes)", was all Ras Fela could muster.

"Honderd en zestig jaar! (One hundred and sixty years!)", questioned Old Layla in astonishment.

"En je zult alles vergeten (And you will forget everything)", informed Ras Fela, they held one another and wept for lost time.

***

Layla looked at Rasta Rabbit with tears in her eyes, actually able to visualize this moment of loss was beyond words.

Once, past-Layla resumed her composure and able to speak, her voice sounded wounded and full of remorse.

***

"Dus, ik zal u niet meer zien totdat tot 2010? (So, I won't see you again until 2010?)", Old Layla managed.

"Nay (No)", Ras Fela exclaimed, "we zullen elkaar weer ontmoeten maar niet en Rastaland tot 2010 (we shall meet again, but not in Rastaland until 2010)", informed Ras Fela.

"And when I return I will not know you?," Old Layla expressed, speaking what 'the others' would consider the 'King's' language, knowing her brother spoke all languages, "Not know that Thee Creator has blessed me with insurmountable competence, deities for parents and true loyalty as my broer" Old Layla's eyes were wide and full of tears as she came to this conclusion.

"Tell me some thing's you like to remember sister?" asked Ras Fela, directing the focus of their conversation to love of life not defeat and sadness.

"The warmth of my realm, the beauty of the beings and the land, Grandma Topoah's cooking, Grandpa Boaz's bluntness, Auntie Cleo's eyelashes on my cheeks, Daddies Den, where I yearned to smoke the ganja of truth with the Lions of Law. Mama's generosity, her kindness, her power. And I never want to forget you brother! Spending seventy years with me on another planet! As someone else! Learning their language, ways, and evils! Guiding and protecting me! My loyal companion! My brother!" Old Layla hugged Ras Fela once again and he too began to weep, startling bird watchers and children alike as he cried unashamed in his sister's arms.

***

"We were really close" stated Present Layla starring glassy eyed at Ras Fela and the older version of herself embracing.

"Yes. You still are dear one! Your bond is something time can never compromise." Rasta Rabbit.

***

Ras Fela straightened up and they calmed one another,

both understanding they could not allow their fear to overcome their reality.

"Winter will not win sister! Victory is righteousness in its physical form, the definition of who we are." Ras Fela.

"You can't do anything to speed up the process?" Old Layla

"No, I know your return will be the year of two thousand ten, but I don't know how we break the curse or how we get you there. I can only see so much in the Future Forest" clarified Ras Fela.

"Will my death be painful?" asked Old Layla.

"No, mom, dad and myself will be there, we will attempt to take you home then, but from what I have saw in the future it will not work. I'm sorry but we will continue to fight and undo all Winter is trying to accomplish. And we will never stop until you're home and she has been abolished" Ras Fela.

"Come brother, let's spend our last day together smoking down the canal's, not crying in Amstel Park!" exclaimed Old Layla standing and pulling Ras Fela into an embrace, holding hands and one another up right, they walked towards their boat on the Amstel River.

***

Rasta Rabbit shouted 'Lomo' and he and Layla were back on Earth near the weed stalk.

"Were back?" questioned Layla.

"We never left!" Rasta Rabbit.

"Wow, how did she pass? Was she sick?" Layla asked.

"You" Rasta Rabbit said pointing at Layla, "Spent the day with your brother on the river, you went to the theatre and dinner. And your heart stopped that night at ten thirty p.m., you died peacefully in your sleep, your family at your side." Rasta Rabbit concluded.

"And they could not break the curse? Is Winter more powerful than Osiris and Isis, Ras and Cleo?" Layla.

"It's not about being powerful; it was Winter's insidious infiltration of Rastaland. Being a first-class wizard herself she inaugurated the greatest conjuror in Rastaland, he poured all of her hate into the curse. The curse could not be broken because Winter placed a piece of her and your essence into the binding spell; so one of you will have to die to break it. This being our seventh and final chance to sever ties, the eighth time would cancel out the spell and you would have been stuck on Earth forever or until Winter decided to come there and kill you or bring you to Rastaland and control your mind along with ours! She wants us as her robots, she's already created a few!" said Rasta Rabbit.

"Pure evil! As if taking me from all I know wasn't enough!" Layla.

"Shall we visit another life? Maybe these visuals will stimulate your memory?" said Rasta Rabbit with hope in his voice.

"Yes, I would love to remember all of the things the older me feared to forget!" Layla.

"Okay! Well I'm getting really high off these past life spliffs. So, you will have to smoke and blow, you can also decide which life you would like to visit." said Rasta Rabbit.

"Past life spliff?" Layla asked, face scrunched into a ball.

"Of course! We have the most potent ganja in the cosmos here in Rastaland! Our tittles of genus or cannabis describe there affects, so you would smoke cozy ganja to relax, future ganja to see the future and…"

"A past life joint to see the past", interrupted Layla, obviously knowing what was next.

"So where to?", asked Rasta Rabbit handing Layla the joint.

"Where were my lives?", Layla inquired.

"The lives where you remembered the most, that influenced your loved ones to pull dialects from those countries and make them our own were Holland which you've saw, Africa and Cuba." informed Rasta Rabbit.

"Africa" Layla.

"Here" said Rasta Rabbit handing Layla the joint.

"How does it work?" Layla asked.

"Inhale this moment and exhale the past, you only need to hit it once while chanting your destination or visualizing it in your mind, saying *lomo* will bring you back to the present moment." elaborated Rasta Rabbit.

"So inhale while chanting Africa in my mind and blow?" questioned Layla.

"You've rephrased what I said perfectly, now let's see if you can carbon copy me physically." teased Rasta Rabbit.

"Here it goes!" said Layla smiling at Rasta Rabbit's snide remark, she took the spliff, noticing this was the first time she disconnected from Rasta Rabbit since this session began.

"Ill need a light." Layla said holding out her hand for one.

"Nope, no fire is needed, just inhale and blow." instructed Rasta Rabbit.

"You don't need fire to light your joints?" asked Layla.

"Not with this particular ganja, your soul ignites the plant of the past, present and future" Rasta Rabbit said wrapping his arm around Layla's.

Layla began to chant Africa in her head placing the spliff between her lips she inhaled deeply. The herb tasted so potent it was as if she was sucking on a weed leaf. Her lips tingled and so did her brain! She held the superb smoke in until she could no longer. Upon exhaling she felt a wave of heat. Before her eyes the forest they were in became a market street!

There were trees on one side of the street and venders on the other. She and Rasta Rabbit stood beneath a gold canopy made of branches and leaves intertwined with steel becoming a metal flower.

"We are in Dar Es Salaam, Tanzania Africa," said Rasta Rabbit, Layla looked down at there arms folded around one another she holding him in this past moment.

She felt high! She wanted to dance, sing, sleep and eat all at once, from one toke, no wonder Rasta Rabbit didn't want to continue smoking. This was some of that 'hit it and quit it weed!'

"Dar Es Salaam, literally meaning 'the abode of peace' A flourishing piece of paradise in East Africa!" Rasta Rabbit begin, squeezing Layla's arm before continuing.

"The year is 1823, you have been affected by slavery immensely, raped and abused by your own kind, witnessed your ancestor's sale their legacy into slavery. And you know you don't belong here! That these kings and queens know not who they are so they sale themselves literally! You know you are a queen and Osiris is here to reinstate that belief, your family has not been able to reach you since your last life in 1777. Now slavery is amiss in Africa, eroding the very core of the inhabitants here. Winter is aware of this and made it extremely difficult to find you in this life. In most of your past lives you lived as royalty on Earth, your life in Holland for example and the life you lead on Earth in the present was pretty nice? Right?" asked Rasta Rabbit.

Layla reflected on her posh existence in Ohio, her parents and boyfriend providing for her, smoking weed all day and going to school, yes she did have a pretty nice life.

"Yes" Layla responded.

"Well this life was extremely hard on your soul, you wanted to commit suicide many times but knew your family would come for you and you waited for that moment, we will visit it now." concluded Rasta Rabbit.

They stood on a busy market street, vendors sold fruit, vegetables and meat from their tents. Layla watched white men moving herds of Africans to and from the auction block off to her left. The slaves had chains around their necks, shackled together by their hips and ankles. A white man holding the chain pulled them behind him.

A crowd of white men were gathered around the auction block deliberating in English, Afrikaans and Swahili. Layla noticed a black chariot approaching, the striking coach was trimmed in gold and pulled by four white horses. Instinctively Layla knew this was her father Osiris arriving, she said so to Rasta Rabbit.

"That's Osiris isn't it?" asked Layla pointing at the arriving wagon.

"Si Princesa, you have recognized your father in the past and present I see." smirked Rasta Rabbit.

Layla watched her past self yank her counterparts along with her. Layla had noticed the wholly headed version of herself before, but when the wagon came to a stop, the woman started to pull and yank everyone in the chariots direction. The white man that was leading her herd was pulling them in the opposite direction of the wagon. The white man began to yell and direct his overseers to control the inconsolable woman with a whip.

Osiris, a white man in this life, jumped down and ran towards the commotion.

Layla and Rasta Rabbit followed close behind him as he ran passed them to meet the disturbance.

***

"Sorry Sire, I am Sir Lance de Grote the third, here to pay whatever amount you see fit for my kaffir slave girl. She is a personal favorite of mine and her selling was a trite error." said Osiris addressing the white men.

"She sho seems attached to you as well, de Grote? You say?" asked the white man.

"Yes, Lance will be fine and you are?" asked Osiris extending his hand.

"Walter Young." said white man Walter refusing to shake Osiris's hand.

"Yes, she has worked for my family for years, she recognized my wagon of course, your price Mr. Young?" asked Osiris.

"You wanna pay a pretty penny for this ugly nigger? Shit we have slaves on the farm we headed to that's younger and prettier than she is!" said Walter

"It's not about looks or money Mr. Young" said Osiris.

"I can see it's not about money!" stated Walter looking Osiris up and down, Osiris looked extremely distinguished and wealthy in his black suit, cane and top hat. Walter

compared his daily rags he wore as overseer to Osiris's tailored suit and knew that money was no object.

"Five thousand for the nigger de Grote!" answered Walter.

"I'll pay seven" said Osiris, he turned and nodded at his driver, who began to walk towards them with a suitcase.

"So may my driver settle our debt while you unchain my slave please?" Osiris asked.

"Sure thang de Grote!" Walter stated smiling exposing tobacco stained teeth.

While Walter unchained Past Layla, Osiris' driver paid the second overseer. Once unchained she walked slowly towards Osiris, you could see in her face the relief she felt. Osiris guided her by her chained wrist back to his wagon.

***

"Ok," exclaimed Rasta Rabbit "You must hit the spliff again to get us to the next moment." He instructed.

"Alright," Layla said still holding the joint in her hand.

She inhaled it deeply, watching the tip light up magically at the end, her lungs wrapping around the smoke, the smoke wrapping around her mind. Once she exhaled, the market place and auction block faded away, evaporating into the atmosphere. They were now in the desert, the sand was red.

Her and Rasta Rabbit on one side beneath a large tree, the Kilimanjaro mountain took up the other side. A river ran down the middle, Osiris and Past Layla exited the carriage, Osiris clapped his hands once; the chariot and driver disappeared, he clapped his hands twice and became the African King he was, towering over Past Layla dressed in tribal gear, diamond crown atop his head, his token necklace with the revolving symbol upon his neck. No longer the Dutch man he came as Osiris kissed Past Layla's cheek and her chains faded, her bleeding wrist and whipped back healed. She stood in a black lace gown trimmed in Rasta colors around the borders, her diamond plated shoes sparkled in the sun light.

***

"I'm sorry I took so long Princesa!" Osiris began, "Winter has made it excessively laborious to past through any portals that lead to Earth. She placed a block on this planet, once you enter a portal you can get so twisted and turned around, sent to different realms and dimensions. That's why I'm alone, your mother and brother send their love!" Osiris concluded pulling Layla in his arms warmly.

"It has been horrific father!" Past Layla wept into his shoulder.

"I know! The affects of slavery today will haunt the future Africans of tomorrow." Osiris sadly stated.

"It will never end?" questioned Past Layla in astonishment.

"The wazungu (white man in Swahili) will cease using whips, recoil from physical abuse. The mind is what will remain enslaved! Like Winter, the white man is fully aware of the power of one's mind, your ideas of who you are, what you will become, is all you have. So, if someone controls your mind they control you! They have turned Africans against each other with skin color, separating the field and house slaves, disposing of African religion, rituals, language. Africans will arrive in America and Europe stripped of everything but their souls! After the civil rights movement, wars and even an African American

president, the Africans of the western world of the future who are slaves today, will still feel the whip of these master's of yestermorn." Osiris.

"Why! Why father?!" Past Layla begin to scream.

"Calm yourself Layla!" Osiris spoke embracing her once more.

"You could never understand what it is to be a slave father! They tell us we are not human, when only something inhuman could commit such acts! Are they human father?" Past Layla asked.

"Who child?" asked Osiris.

"The wazungu? (white man)" Past Layla.

"Yes, they are from this world." Osiris replied.

"They are not aliens or..." Past Layla began questioning further.

"Why do you think that?" inquired Osiris.

"The way they divide, rule, and conquer us! It's as if they have a personal vendetta! Born and breed to hate, bringing their children to watch us burn! Every culture has had slaves, but none has gone to this extreme!" Past Layla said breathlessly summoning up her experience as a slave.

"The white man is extreme! He is a brilliant being! He knows he is a God! He conquered by utilizing trickery, incorporating God's name so he could sleep at night! Called themselves missionaries! Whipping and killing you in the name of God! But the smartest thing he did today that resonates in the minds of every African tomorrow is corrupt your thoughts of yourself. Mind control, hence

Winter!" said Osiris pointing to Past Layla's head.

"She knows I'm a slave and she made it harder for you to get to me! I hate her!" Layla spat at Winter's cruelty.

"Hate is a strong emotion but I understand and your right, Winter is evil manifested and must be stopped." said Osiris.

"Please kill me father" Asked Past Layla.

"Oh! My child!" said Osiris.

They hugged one another crying in each other's arms for a long time.

***

During their past journey Layla, who had tears in her eyes as well squeezed Rasta Rabbits arm tight, reflecting on Osiris's words, He was right! Even in two thousand ten African Americans were suffering from the repercussions of slavery she witnessed there. Black fathers were like breeders, most were absent. The black woman is alone, black family dead, black men incarcerated the new plantations! Darker blacks hated and ridiculed for the color of their skin. Thinking about the state of the world today, Layla could identify the 'Willie Lynch Letter' handprint on her culture. She began to cry harder, Rasta Rabbit kissed her cheek for comfort.

***

"Father you must kill me!" Yelled Past Layla, disrupting the silence and breaking the embrace with Osiris.

When Osiris didn't answer, Past Layla continued.

"I know you could make me white, give me a better life! But what about our people? I can not live here and watch

them suffer and I can not suffer beside them! I'm weak! They are so resilient! Though it's too late as we curse the day they made us slaves, as they move us with their ships, kill us with their guns, whip us to death in the name of their God! These Africans hold on! As I held on for you, what will become of Mama Africa father?" Asked Layla.

"After war, slavery and apartheid there will be a disease called AIDS that will devastate her! Her people will be on foreign soil and some will not want to be associated with Africa, never yearn to be African. Generations of her people will never return, her currency worthless, her streets will be ravished with defeat, but her heart will remain strong!" replied Osiris.

"Kill me father! To leave me here to die is an intolerable death!" Past Layla.

"I despise that I have to disguise myself as a white man to roam this planet safely. Winter would love to know that! But it breaks my heart that these beings have made life so hellacious you would rather die than live out your remaining days here. I know what you have been through and it killed us we could not get here to stop it. Winter wanted you to live a long life as a slave, I am here to end that. I love you." completed Osiris.

He kissed Past Layla on the lips, she smiled. Then he sucked her life out, when he blew her being in the air, her essence hovered above them, it looked at Present Layla and Rasta Rabbit before floating away.

***

"Did you see that!? It looked at me! Was that my soul?" Layla asked Rasta Rabbit.

"No, the essence of you, is the only way to explain it, your soul lies within that." interpreted Rasta Rabbit.

"It looked at me!" said Layla.

"You acknowledged your presence." answered Rasta Rabbit.

***

Osiris's crying stopped Layla from asking her next question.

Osiris held the limp body of Past Layla and wept. He allowed his emotions to flow as he crushed his daughter to his chest. Crying out before speaking with God, lifting his head to the sky he spoke;

"God, I know you will not allow Winter to succeed! Please show us the way to retrieving our daughter and bringing her home! Please send your swift mercy to our ailing ancestors here! May you guide and protect us all eternally! Nema." And with those words Osiris disappeared.

***

"Lomo" Rasta Rabbit said to Layla "Say lomo."

"Lomo!" shouted Layla "Sorry I forgot to say the password to get us back!" she said sadly affected by her African past life.

"Don't be sad Princesa, these reviews are to give you strength! Remembering who you are is powerful! Empowering!" Rasta Rabbit said to soothe Layla.

Moving away from Rasta Rabbit, now that they were back on Earth, Layla began walking towards the stalk, her arms reaching out to touch it!

"Stop!" Rasta Rabbit shouted walking up to Layla and spinning her around to face him.

"You'll end up back in Ivory Heights, Winter's domain in

Rastaland." Rasta Rabbit informed Layla.

"I can't view another past life; I don't want to see my next life if it's that horrible!" hollered Layla breaking down in tears.

"You have low points in every life! What we just observed was severe, yet if you keep walking in darkness you will soon see the light! The objective is to keep walking!" said Rasta Rabbit encourage to Layla, rubbing her back in an effort to console her.

"I'm so tired of being reminded that we were slaves! They never show when we were Kings and Queens!" bawled Layla turning her back on the stalk and Rasta Rabbit.

"They have forgotten who they are! That's how they become enslaved in the first place! You are a Princesa! Future Queen of Rastaland! You too have fallen under the spell of memory loss! Your condition was caused by the hands of another and so was theirs. As the Africans of today must fight to regain their rightful place, so must you! Discovering who you are, reviewing your past, remembering, these are the first steps towards liberation!" related Rasta Rabbit.

Layla pondered his words in silence. Hearing and reading about slavery was nothing compared to being in the energy of those times. She did not blame her past self for seeking death rather than live dead! She contemplated returning to her boring life in Ohio, her posh existence. Yet that feeling of wanting more than existing thrived in her gut and she knew in her heart she was the Queen of this Rasta Realm; she must summon the strength in her soul to continue.

"Was my life in Spain as difficult as it was in Africa?" questioned Layla turning to face Rasta Rabbit.

You mean Cuba? And no" answered Rasta Rabbit.

"Cuba?" asked Layla.

"Yes, its where your memory began to fade the most, your

life with your mother Isis." said Rasta Rabbit.

"Okay, who is smoking this time?" asked Layla.

"Are you still high?" asked Rasta Rabbit.

"No, my high was blown by slavery!" said Layla.

"I feel you" chuckled Rasta Rabbit, "So" he continued "Let's lock arms and both smoke. Just chant Cuba in your mind, hold in your smoke until I have inhaled, I will lift my free hand and count to three, when my third finger raises blow out your smoke." instructed Rasta Rabbit gesturing with his hand, ensuring Layla understood.

"Okay" answered Layla nodding her head.

"Let's smoke" said Rasta Rabbit locking arms with Layla.

Layla put the spliff that she held in her hand into her mouth and pulled. She handed the joint to Rasta Rabbit and he inhaled. Lifting his free left arm, he counted to three by holding up one finger at a time, when he raised his third finger they exhaled in unison.

The wind pulled the smoke from their lips, blanketing them in its aroma, converting the landscape from a forest to a Cuban village. They stood in the middle of a street that held shack houses nestled close together aligning both sides of the road.

Layla was afraid of the wild dogs that ran passed and jumped when one came too close.

"Hey, you're fine they can't see you! So, they can't bite you! And don't jump away from me, remember we must remain connected to remain in past memory together and I can't have you back on Earth wandering around touching stalks!" reprimanded Rasta Rabbit.

"I get it" Layla said squeezing both arms tightly around Rasta Rabbits.

"There you are!" said Rasta Rabbit pointing to a teenage girl exiting one of the colorful shanty homes, the houses all had steel roofs and vegetation for backyards. She waved to a man up on the roof and continued walking to the back of the house.

"Let's follow her" Rasta Rabbit said and followed Past Layla behind her home. She was bending down pulling weeds from the mariposa (butterfly flowers) flower that bloomed there. Cuban orchids and other beautiful plants made their home in her garden, further down the hill there was a small vegetable patch.

Past Layla was lovely in her simple flower dress, at home barefoot and at ease cultivating the Earth around her.

"We are in Havana, Cuba's capital, its 1957. Your family came to you three more times since your past life in 1823, one time in Paris in 1937. This past life in Cuba in 1957and this present and seventh time in two thousand ten. Now back to the past; It's 1957 Che Guevara cast his assault on Cuba from Mexico in 1956, were in the mist of the Cuban Revolution. So, no one knew if Che was alive after that attack until 1957, when an interview by Herbert Matthews detailed his well being in the New York Times.

Your mother…," Rasta Rabbit said pointing at Isis coming up the hill past the vegetable garden.

He continued, "…Was apart of the revolution in this life, assisting in their fight on Earth while protecting her daughter, seeking away to take you to Rastaland. Your mother always knew there was a loop hole in Winter's curse and she was right! Her persistence led us to this moment." completed Rasta Rabbit.

Layla was caught up in Isis approach, Isis was a tall dark Indian woman in this life. She had on a dress made up of colorful beads, traces of the beads were in her hair that came to her ankles. Her smooth skin was moca in motion, Layla loved her jewelry and beaded shoes, Mother Nature in the flesh.

She walked up to Past Layla who had her back to her replanting flowers.

***

"Layla" Isis called her name.

"Hola! Soy Anita (Hi, I'm Anita)" Greeted Past Layla smiling up at Isis.

Isis looked at her daughter and tears came to her eyes, rolling unchecked down her cheeks, ignored by Isis who stared at her daughter in disbelief.

"Por qué estás llorando? Qué está mal? (Why are you crying? What's wrong?)" Asked Past Layla.

"Nunca lo entenderías? (You would never understand)" spoke Isis walking away and covering her face, she began crying harder.

Past Laya, Rasta Rabbit and Present Layla pursued her, staying close on her heels as she exited the garden walking back down the hill towards the farm.

Past Layla ran up to her, grabbing her shoulder, spinning Isis around to face her.

"Qué es? Raúl te ha robado? (What is it? Has Raul stolen from you?)" Asked Past Layla, referring to her thieving uncle.

"No, mis lágrimas son por ti, usted no sabe quién soy. (No, my tears are because of you, you not knowing who I am.)" explained Isis.

"Un revolucionario? (A revolutionary?)" asked Past Layla fingering the small Che button pinned to Isis dress.

"Sí y tu madre (Yes and your mother)" Isis.

"Mi madre está en el sofá dentro de la casa con un estómago agrio eructar pedos y maldecir a mi padre! (My mother is on the couch inside the house with a sour stomach, belching farts and cussing out my father)!" Past Layla.

***

Rasta Rabbit and Present Layla giggled picturing this description, standing a few feet away listening to the conversation.

***

Isis smiled placing both of her hands on either side of Past Layla's face.

"Soy tu madre. (I'm your mother.)" Isis said.

***

When her hands touched Past Layla's face, Rasta Rabbit and Present Layla could see the waves of energy transferring from Isis' hands into Past Layla's mind. Past Layla closed her eyes for a few seconds, when she opened her eyes again she grabbed Isis hands and stepped back.

***

"Mamá! (Mama!)" Past Layla said in disbelief and recognition, looking at the backs of her sparkling hands in gratitude.

"Si. Te he hecho recordar quién eres, si solo por el momento. (Yes. I have caused you to remember who you are, if only for the moment.)" Isis.

"Cómo es esto possible? ¿Estoy teniendo un ataque de nervios? (How is this possible? Am I having a nervous

breakdown?)" questioned Past Layla.

***

Present Layla recognized this feeling of disbelief and panic, she was living it right now!

***

"No luche contra su hija! (Don't fight it daughter!)," advised Isis, "Abre tu mente y di tu nombre! (Open your mind and say your name!)," she instructed.

Past Layla looked around her, running her eyes over the scenery as if it was her first time seeing her environment. She looked at her hands and arms, touching herself like a wild woman in dubiety.

"Tu nombre. (Your name)," demanded Isis.

"Lay-la" Past Layla said speaking her name as if she was afraid of it.

"Si. Layla, eso es lo que eres. (Yes. Layla, that's who you are)," Isis.

"Mamá! (Mama!)" Shouted Layla hugging Isis close.

"Si hija. (Yes daughter)," said Isis.

"Oh! ¡Dios mío! ¡Esta funcionando! El hechizo de invierno está funcionando! ¡Si no me hubieras tocado, nunca me hubiera acordado! ¿Quién puede decir que en la próxima vida lo haré? (Oh! My God! It's working! Winter's spell is working! If you hadn't touched me I would have never remembered! Who's to say in the next life I will!)," said Past Layla in fright.

***

Rasta Rabbit looked at Present Layla, his eyes said that Past Layla was right and this was the life she referred to in two thousand ten, and Layla nodded her head in understanding and turned her attention back to the past.

***

"¡El invierno no prosperará! Ella recibirá su justa recompensa! Dios realiza un seguimiento de todas las acciones; consecuencia es la venganza de la vida! Somos soldados en una revolución! Al igual que Fidel y el Che. (Winter will not and can not prosper! She will receive her just reward! God keeps track of all actions; consequence is life's revenge! We are soldiers in a revolution! Just like Fidel and Che)," Isis said pointing to her button.

"Ella ha tomado todo! ¡Mi mente! ¡Mi vida contigo! ¡Mi poder! (She's taken everything! My mind! My life with you! My power!)," spoke Past Layla defeated.

"Ella nunca puede tomar su poder. (She can never take your power!)," said Isis.

"Mi mente es mi poder. (My mind is my power!)," corrected Past Layla.

Mother and daughter looked at one another, each at a loss for words, seeking a resolution.

"¿Alguna vez veré a papá? Ras? ¿Cuándo terminará esta vida de pesadillas? (Will I ever see Daddy? Ras? When will this lifetime of nightmares end?)," questioned Past Layla.

"¡Te llevaremos a casa! (We will get you home!)," replied Isis wrapping her arms around Past Layla for comfort.

"¡La destruiré! (I will destroy her!)," said Past Layla

*breaking their embrace to look her mother in the eyes.
"¡Lo recuerdo todo ahora! Plagas! ¡Esclavitud! ¡Ahora
Cuba! ¡Nacido en la pobreza de padres abusivos y
abusador de un tío! (I remember it all now! Plagues!
Slavery! Now Cuba! Born into poverty to abusive parents
and a molester for an uncle!)," Past Layla yelled.*

*"¡Oh! (Oh!)," Isis covered her mouth with both hands and
began to whimper.*

*"¡Sé que encontraremos la manera de llevarme a casa!
¡Puedo sentirlo! Pero ella me ha tomado en cuenta y
colocó mi cuerpo en el infierno por ahora. (I know we will
find a way to get me home! I can feel it! But she's taken my
mind and placed my body in hell for now!)," reflected Past
Layla.*

"¡No! (No!)," Isis said her voice low and deliberate.

*"¡Sí! ¡Si ella tiene! Y aunque sabemos que el futuro es mi
liberación, ¡no soy libre en este momento! En este
momento, soy una chica cubana, perdida en un país en
guerra en un planeta que crea su propia desaparición,
¡con seres que viven conscientemente muertos! Ellos
consumen la muerte aquí! ¡Y solo empeorarán!
Encontrarán una forma de destruir este planeta, por lo
tanto, Atlantas, ¡descubrirán otra manera de borrar todo
lo bueno! ¡Pero! ¡Pero dejaré este lugar, este pozo, este
planeta! (Yes! Yes, she has! And though we know the
future holds my release, I am not free in this moment! In
this moment, I'm a Cuban girl, lost in a country at war on
a planet creating its own demise, with beings consciously
living dead! They consume death here! And they will only
get worse! They will find a way to destroy this planet,
hence Atlantas, they will discover another way to*

obliterate everything good! But! But I will leave this place, this pit, this planet!)," exclaimed Past Layla.

"¡¡Sí lo haré!! ¡Y volveré a casa! ¡Casa! ¡Cuánto anhelo volver a vivir allí, sentir la brisa de Rasta, cabalgar, correr, caminar por las calles de nuestro reino, desde que tenía seis años soñaba con dirigir Hijas de Osiris, mi ciudad! ¡Ahora quiero cultivar orquídeas cubanas en mi laberinto! ¡Debería estar inspeccionando reinos, aprendiendo mi lugar en el sol, cambiando de forma, fumando la mejor ganga del universo con Ras Fela en su castillo! ¡Aquí no se trata de absurdas monstruosidades humanas! ¡Ella me ha colocado aquí y he estado aquí por décadas! Viviendo solo para morir a vivir de nuevo! ¡Incluso cuando me vengo desmoronando su corazón ella todavía ha logrado tomar tanto tiempo de mí! ¡La malvada bruja! (Yes I will!! And I'll return home! Home! How I long to live there again, to feel the Rasta breeze, to ride, run, walk along the streets of our realm, since I was six I dreamed of running Daughters of Osiris, my city! Now I want to grow Cuban orchids in my labyrinth! I should be inspecting realms, learning my place in the sun, shape shifting, smoking the best ganga in the universe with Ras Fela in his castle! Not here dealing with ludicrous human monstrosities! She has placed me here and I've been here for decades! Living just to die to live again! Even when I get my revenge by crumbling her heart she has still succeeded in taking so much time from me! The evil witch!)," Past Layla yelped grabbing her head, the onslaught of emotions affecting her physically.

Isis went to Past Layla encircling her with her arms and love.

"Es el hechizo de la memoria que se desvanece, pronto me olvidarás y te convertirás en Anita Guteraz. (The spell of remembrance is fading, soon you will forget me and become Anita Guteraz.), " Isis explained.

"Sé que eres hija enojada. (I know you're angry daughter)," Isis continued, "¡Pero debes permanecer enfocado! ¡Te amo! Y ese amor supera cualquier maldición, mi amor, ¡nuestro amor por ti es el remedio! ¡No nos detendremos hasta que te llevemos a casa! (But you must remain focused! I love you! And that love surpasses any curse, my love our love for you is the remedy! We will not stop until we get you home!)," Isis encouraged.

"Cuando regrese, ¿me llevarás al sol? Enséñame a permanecer en formación después de cambiar de forma? (When I return, will you take me to the sun? Teach me to stay in formation after shape shifting?)," asked Past Layla, closing her eyes she shape shifted into a beautiful parrot.

"¡Guacamayo cubano, nativo de la isla caribeña, esta especie está extinta! ¡Qué hermoso ser inteligente eres! (A Cuban Macaw, native to the Caribbean Island, this species is extinct! What an intelligent beautiful being you are.), " spoke Isis to Past Layla perched on her forearm, she kissed her beak.

"¿Estás tratando de decir que te extinguirás también? ¡Nunca! Mantenga la fe amor! (Are you trying to say you'll become extinct as well? Never! Keep the faith love!)," Said Isis.

When Past Layla attempted to fly, she became human falling from the sky to her mother's feet. Her clothes were torn and she was unconscious, breathing hard, laying still on the ground.

Isis knelt beside her and wept, she combed her fingers gently through Past Layla's hair, softly rubbing her back. After a few seconds of comforting her, Isis jerked her head up as if she heard something. Staring in the direction of the farm, Isis kissed Past Layla on the cheek, rubbed her hands in the grass three times, meditating silently with closed eyes. When Isis opened her eyes, she spoke the word 'Nema' and disappeared.

***

"What happened? Why did she vanish? And why do they say 'Nema' before disappearing?" Inquired Present Layla.

"She sensed Winter's approach and 'Nema' is Amen backwards on your planet, used in Rastaland to end prayer as well, you have witnessed the King and Queen utilize it in prayer and as a safe word to return home" Rasta Rabbit informed Layla.

"Winter's here?" asked Layla.

"Yes, she is close to Isis, them being sisters and all and she felt the pull of her sister's energy to this planet. Isis vanished to leave no trace of her visit. Winter's just guessing but if she would have had proof that Isis was here she would have done something far worse than what she did." said Rasta Rabbit.

"What did she do?" Layla.

"Hit the joint and watch" instructed Rasta Rabbit.

Layla hit the joint, loving the taste of the pure plant on her tongue. Blowing out the smoke she saw a woman from the house approaching the field near a sleeping Past Layla, where she and Rasta Rabbit stood.

As she came closer Present Layla could see a barefoot

middle aged Cuban woman with black curly shoulder length hair in a red and white polka dot house dress.

"That's Winter concealed as your mother in this life." enlighten Rasta Rabbit.

Past Layla began to stir and come to on the ground, covering her eyes with her hands she rolled over on her back to block out the sun.

Rasta Rabbit and Present Layla observed Winter creeping up on Past Layla, smug frown in place.

***

"Relajante, ¿verdad? (Relaxing, are we?)," said Winter.

"¡Mami! (Mami!)," stated Past Layla.

"¡No Mami! Worky! ¡Se supone que debes podar y sacar malas hierbas de mi jardín! (No Mami! Worky! You're supposed to be pruning and pulling weeds out of my garden!)," Winter yelled.

"Yo soy. (I am)," replied Past Layla.

"¿Cómo se supone que sobreviviremos contigo en tu espalda? ¡Ni siquiera tienes una polla en ti! (How are we supposed to survive with you on your back! You don't even have a dick in you!)," shouted Winter.

Past Layla looked stunned, Winter's last remark snatching any words from her lips.

"¡Qué! ¡Nada más que decir para ti que no sea Mami y yo! (What! Nothing more to say for yourself other than Mami and I am!)," taunted Winter.

Past Layla got to her feet and tried to walk past Winter to the garden. Winter shoved her hand in her stomach preventing her from going, pushing her backwards.

"¿Qué? El taco de Paco no es suficiente para que te acuestes boca arriba. Tienes que joder en mi tiempo también? (What? Paco's taco isn't enough beef for you to lie on your back for? You got to fuck around on my time too?)," Winter yelled, spittle flying from her chapped lips, referring to Past Layla's molesting uncle.

The pain from Winter's words forced Past Layla's hand into the air across Winter's face, Winter's head bounced back from the impact, yet she remained unfazed.

Seizing Past Layla by the neck, pulling her down to her knees, Past Layla tried to pry Winter's firm grip from her neck, tears coming to her eyes.

As Winter and Past Layla jostled for control of their predicament, Rasta Rabbit pointed out Isis to Present Layla. Isis was suspended in mid air camouflaged as a sunray. Rasta Rabbit pointed to the joint in Present Layla's hand, she handed it to him, exhaling the smoke he drew the outline of Isis in the sky.

Winter pushed Past Layla to the ground, when Past Layla stood and attempted to speak, she couldn't.

"¡He tomado tu voz junto con tu mente! ¡Ahora ni siquiera puedes pedir ayuda! (I have taken your voice along with your mind! Now you can't even call for help!)," mocked Winter laughing.

Her laughter was fake, hollow, bordering hysterical an ear shattering shriek! Citizens begin emptying out onto the streets! Winter begin holding her belly, falling to her knees, collapsing onto her back she rolled in the grass wrapped up in her own private party, roaring with laughter, a mad woman!

Past Layla's family surrounded them, Past Layla could not speak and continued to cry and grab her throat as her family and friends comforted her. When Winter stopped laughing she stopped breathing, taken Past Layla's mother's life as she exited her body.

Past Layla's family began to scream out in fright! Their neighbors consoled them trying to make sense of what they just witnessed! Swathing her mother in cloth her family carried her to the car. Past Layla was escorted to a horse that she was to ride with her cousin to the hospital. Walking towards the animal Past Layla tripped.

"Owww!" She yelped.

Realizing her voice had returned her cousin ran to her side!

"Tu voz ha vuelto? (Your voice is back?)," questioned her cousin.

"Si. (Yes.)," Past Layla responded in awe.

"¿Que pasó? (What happened?)," her cousin asked.

"¡No lo sé! ¡Estaba descansando y Mami salió gritándome! ¡Me ahogó hasta que ya no pude hablar! ¡Entonces también se rió de la muerte! ¡Lo viste con tus propios ojos, Inez! (I don't know! I was resting and Mami came out yelling at me! She choked me till I could no longer speak! Then laughed too death! You saw that with your own eyes Inez!)," said Past Layla.

"Oh! ¡Dios mío! ¡Tenemos que alejarte de aquí! (Oh! My God! We have to get you away from here!)," urgently shouted Inez.

"¿A dónde iría? (Where would I go?)," Past Layla asked.

"Iremos a Maria! ¡Puedes quedarte allí hasta que encontremos algo más! ¡Pero no puedes quedarte aquí! ¡No con tu padre y tu tío! ¿Quién sabe lo que te harían? (We'll go to Maria! You can stay there until we come up with something else! But you can't stay here! Not with your father and uncle! Who knows what they would do to you!)," replied Inez.

"Ella no me protegió! (She didn't protect me!)," stated Past Layla.

"¡Esa es una razón más para irse! (That's even more reason to leave!)," responded Inez.

And without another look back, both girls mounted the horse, heading in the opposite direction of Past Layla's family and the growing crowd.

***

Rasta Rabbit looked at Present Layla,
"Please speak the magic word." prompted Rasta Rabbit.
"Lomo" Spoke Layla remembering the exit word.
They were back in nature's park on Earth where they began.
"So?" said Layla, cuing Rasta Rabbit for more information.
"So?" repeated Rasta Rabbit.
"What happened?" asked Layla.
"Your mother gave you back your voice and you lived at Maria's, a close friend, for awhile. Met a farmer at the local market, became his wife, had his children. You created a family of your own, never looking back on your past family, or that day again, you didn't question the incident with Winter or your mother in that life whom Winter was the puppet master of, you were just elated to be liberated from that situation."

elaborated Rasta Rabbit.

"Winter never found out that my voice returned? Or that I'd run away?" questioned Layla.

"She doesn't care! You could run anywhere you wanted to! On Earth! Your mother was in no rush to get back after that close call with Winter!" said Rasta Rabbit.

"Winter never returned?" Layla asked.

"Why? The damage was done! It didn't matter if you could speak or not! If you left home! If you lived happily ever after! You were on Earth, right where she wanted you! And so much time had past she knew that if your family could have broken the spell and gotten you home they would have! She was comfortable in that fact! She was back in Rastaland concocting ways to take us all out! She has your mind! She's won from her perspective!" said Rasta Rabbit.

"She doesn't have my mind!" hollered Layla into Rasta Rabbits face.

"You no longer have to hold on to me, were out of memory travel!" Rasta Rabbit yelled back while quickly unlocking his arm from hers.

"She doesn't have my mind!" repeated Layla shoving Rasta Rabbit aside, crossing her arms and scowling silmultaneously.

"So what have you learned from your past lives?" Rasta Rabbit said in his best interrogation voice.

"That she doesn't have my mind!" Layla stated smugly.

"Stop being so stubborn Layla! Winter has worked her trick well! You don't remember who you are! Before I came along you wouldn't have known Isis from Winter!" educated Rasta Rabbit.

Layla pondered this statement, surrendering to defeat, she said,

"I learned that I have to seize these moments to make up for the past ones." Layla answered as means of an apology, coming to terms with the confrontation of her mission.

"And?" asked Rasta Rabbit.

"And I still want to smoke the ganja of truth with the Lions of Law as I yearned to in Amsterdam. I want to thank my father for his rescue and execution in Africa. For, I feel the same about that situation now as I did then! And I must confront and destroy Winter for placing me on Earth period!" replied Layla.

"I can feel you starting to believe!" smiled Rasta Rabbit, "Now" he continued, "For the second part of our game; mind and seek! Let's test your newfound courage and belief in who you are!" surmised Rasta Rabbit.

"Alright" agreed Layla.

"Ok, we're going to mind travel through memories, just as I followed you through your past lives and memory, you must follow me through mines. But the object of the game is to find me with your mind before the memory expires," explained Rasta Rabbit and continued, "Drink this potion while chanting my name and only I will be able to read your mind during our venture," he continued.

Rasta Rabbit produced a capsule of pink liquid from his pocket. It reminded Layla of Pepto Bismol! He handed it to Layla who eyed it skeptically before drinking the potion chanting Rasta Rabbit's name, it actually tasted like Sprite.

"Ok, so I have to locate you in my memory?" asked Layla.

"Yes, you must find me without speaking. You can call my name in your head but no talking. The punishment for speaking is being stuck in that moment until I find you; and you'll have about three minute per memory. If you're too late or once you've found me, we'll always end up here in the forest our starting point. Got it?" asked Rasta Rabbit.

"I think, do I have to say 'Lomo' to end the memory?" asked Layla.

"No, just locating me will be enough," answered Rasta Rabbit.

Rasta Rabbit and Layla held hands, Layla closed her eyes.

***

BEEEEEEEEEEEEEEEEEEEEEEEEEEEEEEEEEEEEEE EEEEEEP

Blared a horn, she was now in the middle of a street intersection. Looking both ways Layla darted onto the nearest side walk. Or what resembled a side walk they were slabs of a floating planet she had to hop onto. She wasn't on earth anymore, where had Rasta Rabbits memory placed her? There was no light, yet everything glowed, the funny shaped citizens and vehicles. The sky was purple and the clouds looked like balloons. She could hear voices in her head, snippets of conversations, some in languages she didn't understand. She hears him call her name in her mind, she looks around at the other beings but none are Rasta Rabbit.

"Where are you Rabbit?" asks a perplexed Layla in her mind.

"Look to your left" says Rasta Rabbit in Layla's head.

Layla, amid the beings hopping to and fro on the odd slabs, felt like she would if she were downtown in any major city at rush hour, she sees a pair of Rabbit ears roll by one of the peculiar shaped beings about fifty inhabitants ahead of her. She yells "Rasta Rabbit" before remembering to think his name. When she says his name the atmosphere fades away and they are back in the forest holding hands.

***

"Wow" yells Layla.

"Again and this time no speaking! If you do you will be stuck in memory for a few seconds before I can get you out," warns Rasta Rabbit.

***

Layla opened her eyes and looked around what appeared to be an open field of hay and grass. The air was humid, she began sweating. She saw a tractor approaching her, as it got closer she realized the driver was not human and that it was not driving a tractor but riding a furry beast on four legs, coming straight at her full throttle! Layla tried to run for what felt like forever her first step, she could barely breathe, her lungs expanding yet she could collect no O2.

Whatever planet she was on did not have oxygen for humans. As soon as she put one foot in front of the other she was out of breath. Just when she thought she'd pass out and remain stuck in this nightmare forever, she spotted some bunny ears darting through what she assumed was grass, the blades felt like plastic. She followed the ears through a maze of the tall plastic grass, the Rabbit warns Layla in her head not to stare into the eyes of the beings posted against the walls of plastic grass. Afraid Layla thinks 'Rasta Rabbit' and the atmosphere fades away, once again they are back in the forest holding hands.

***

"Wow," exclaims Layla out of breath.

"Again," shouts Rasta Rabbit.

***

Layla materialized in a vestibule, she follows voices through the foyer that emptied into a patio. Two white rabbits were having a mental conversation in the garden off to the left of the porch.

"She's not the right Layla," Rabbit One.

"She is she would have never made it this far if she weren't" Rabbit Two.

"She's too bovine and dawdling to be our Layla" Rabbit One.

"Well that just means the White Witch did a great job erasing her memory!" Rabbit Two.

"Excuse me" interrupted Layla forgetting not to speak.

"Didn't Hoot tell your ass not to speak during mind travel?" Rabbit One yelled.

"My ass? What a filthy mouth you have for a Rabbit" Layla.

"I'm a Rabbit not a kid! And I wouldn't have cussed if you'd followed directions!" Rabbit One.

"Where is Rasta Rabbit?" Layla asks.

"What part of mind and seek says you can talk and 'ask' about who you're seeking?" Rabbit One.

"What part of mind and seek made you such a rude Rabbit?" asks an indignant Layla.

"Stop asking dumb questions missy! You only have a few seconds left to discover Hoot." Rabbit One.

And with that both rabbits sprinted off deeper into the

garden, Layla ran behind them into the grassy field she went. She stopped by a tree shaped like a tear drop, she spotted Rasta Rabbit a few feet ahead of her, but instead of shouting his name aloud as she had done before, she whispered his name in her mind, walking over to him and grabbing his paw.

"Don't speak you'll ruin the moment and since you spoke earlier we must stand here for a moment," thought Rasta Rabbit. Layla heard his thoughts loud and clear in her mind. She looked out and over the field, watching the sun make love to the sky, not minding being forced to stand there and enjoy the view. After several seconds, Rasta Rabbit clapped his paws and they were back in the forest.

***

"You did well my pet! You must remember not to talk when you're in memory. Use your mind and you'll be fine, and this is just the beginning of things you must attain. But you're well on your way Princesa! Now with our minds warmed up, good energy flowing and me at your side, do you think you could get us back to Rastaland Princesa?" asked Rasta Rabbit.

"I'll try Hoot, I'll try" said Layla.

Holding hands, they walked towards the weed stalk.

"Can't the stalk just suck us back there?" asked Layla.

"Yeah, but as I explained when you tried to touch it before, we'd be back at the entrance to Rastaland, where you entered, we need to enter through the labyrinth." Rasta Rabbit answered.

"Why couldn't I think myself there when I first arrived in Rastaland?" questioned Layla.

"You didn't believe you could! One of the many reasons I brought you to Earth was for you to believe us back to

Rastaland." replied Rasta Rabbit.

Layla grabbed Rasta Rabbits paws, clearing her mind and picturing the labyrinth, Layla went back to her earliest memory of the maze. Squeezing Rasta Rabbit as hard and as tight as she could, Layla stepped into her mind and hoped for the best.

■■

CHAPTER SIX SHAPE SHIFTER

Layla opened her eyes to find herself holding Rasta Rabbits paws in her labyrinth.

"To the clouds" said Rasta Rabbit, he then begins to levitate.

"You can fly too?" asked an excited Layla, watching Rasta Rabbit merge with the sky.

"You can too! But first what color is my finger?" asked Rasta Rabbit holding his paws behind his back.

"I don't know but in my mind, I see a rainbow" replied Layla.

"Correct!" exclaimed Rasta Rabbit "What's my favorite animal?" he continued.

"I would say rabbits but in my head, I see a herd of elephants!" replied Layla.

"Exactly!" laughed Rasta Rabbit.

"So here in Rastaland I'm telepathic?" asked Layla.

"You are whatever you want to be here in Rastaland! Yet the beings here can block you from hearing their thoughts, send you pictures instead of thoughts like I did, or trick you if you're not careful. That's why it's important to know my voice and to know that this labyrinth is yours! Appropriately named 'Layla's Labyrinth' nothing will ever harm you in this place of peace your family has created for you! Now that we're done with our memory lesson, you have one half moon before the first full moon and the completion of your first task! So now we must trek to Ivory Heights where the White Witch resides.

You must complete your initial task, discovering the Witches weakness!" explained Rasta Rabbit.

"So what is the White Witches weakness? Black men?" laughs Layla.

"Please spare me your bigotry! We are in a fight for our minds!" angrily stated Rasta Rabbit.

"Ok! You're so serious all of a sudden, but like the white rabbit in your memory said, how do you know that I'm the right Layla?" Layla asked.

"We've tracked you since your inception, as you saw, seven life times. Now in this life before you turn twenty-one and your powers increase to new heights, I must train you so that when the time comes you'll claim your rightful place as Princesa of Rastaland!" explained Rasta Rabbit.

"So I've always been the Princesa of Rastaland and didn't know?" questions Layla.

"Yes, if Winter were to have her way you would never know" Rasta Rabbit, "As you've witnessed we've tracked you over decades! As you said in your Cuban life, watching you grow, learn, die and start all over again. We tried but God allowed us to bring you home when it really mattered! As I've explained before, this is our seventh and final attempt to recapture you. An eighth attempt would have exhausted our energy, cancelling the spell. Do you understand?" Rasta Rabbit floated down from his hovering spot in the sky, landing in front of Layla.

"Yes, you're saying that if you wouldn't have succeeded in bringing me to Rastaland this time, I would have remained on Earth in purgatory!" answered Layla.

"Exactly! Now I will explain Rasta Time to you so that you will understand how long you've been away and the urgency of thwarting Winter's will now that you're back!"

Rasta Rabbit began, "On Earth, you base time on seconds that become minutes that become hours that become years, decades into centuries. Now, your parent's ancestors are of what indigenous tribe on Earth?" questioned Rasta Rabbit.

"Africa!?" Layla said guessing.

"That's a continent on Earth I said a tribe, which country and ethnicity Princesa?" asked Rasta Rabbit again.

"Egypt!" Layla

"Correct! Egyptian was the answer I was looking for; your name is of Egyptian and Arabic descendant..." said Rasta Rabbit.

"Meaning, dark beauty!" said Layla breaking in with the definition.

"Correct again," Rasta Rabbit smiled and continued, "So when your brother Ras Fela created Rastaland he based time on the Egyptian seasons combined with our moon cycles; Akhet-inundation, Peret-Winter and growth, and Shemuh-The Summer. The moon affects all planets, realms and dimensions, including ours. Your mother named our moon 'La Luna' a Spanish moon in Rasta skies. Every two years on Earth is equivalent to a year cycle in Rastaland. Twenty-four years is equal to one full moon cycle; you understand so far?" asked Rasta Rabbit.

"I think? What is inundation?" questioned Layla.

"To flood, our rainy season" Rasta Rabbit informed.

"Winter has a season?" asked Layla.

"Yes! On our realm and your planet! And she is her strongest during her season! Your family having a hard time getting to you in your life in Tanzania in 1823, for example." said Rasta Rabbit.

"Oh! My God! What season are we in now!?" asked Layla now fully comprehending the deadline she was up against.

"Precisely my 'time frame' point." stated Rasta Rabbit, "I will now explain your time line! First allow me to show you a chart of our moon cycles so that you clearly see what I'm explaining." said Rasta Rabbit.

Taking Layla by the hand they went deeper into the labyrinth, the leaves opened and moved back to create a walk way, coming alive and welcoming them. Some of the concrete path was covered in drawings and words in lavender, aqua, pink and white paint creating a canvas of the walkway.

Layla briefly wondered if she had drawn them there as a child. After walking a mile deeper in the maze, they came to a wall of flowers.

Flowers that Layla couldn't identify swayed in the breeze, an arrangement of colors and sizes, the sweet odor of rain and lilac grew stronger as they walked closer. Layla could see the grass rising as they got closer.

"Am I still high on the past ganja joints or is the grass rising?" Layla asked Rasta Rabbit.

"You're still high and yes the grass is rising!" Joked Rasta Rabbit, "That Princesa is the gnome Hierba the protector of your labyrinth." explained Rasta Rabbit.

Made of grass, Hierba easily went unseen in the entanglement; he rose two feet before introducing himself.

"Hierba hier halt alsjeblieft! (*Hierba here stop please!*),'" yelled Hierba, frustrated and bothered by their presence, his voice seeming bigger than his height.

"What did he say?" Layla asked Rasta Rabbit taking in the Gnome made of grass in disbelief.

"His name, Hierba which is Spanish for grass and stop please, you must learn alstublieft, the Dutch word for please, we use it a lot here in Rastaland." expounded Rasta Rabbit to Layla, turning to Hierba he addressed him.

"Jambo! Hierba, we are here to see the timeline." explained Rasta Rabbit to Hierba.

"ik begrijp het niet! (I don't understand)," Hierba yelled throwing his hands in the air.

"Hierba is being difficult" said Rasta Rabbit turning back to face Layla.

"What did he say?" Layla asked again.

"He didn't understand me! I'm tired of giving English lessons." said Rasta Rabbit frustrated.

"Als dit niet Layla is, kan ze de tijdlijn niet zien. (If this is not Layla she will not be able to see the timeline)," said Hierba.

"See I knew he understood me, he just proved it with the point he just made." Rasta Rabbit said to Layla.

"About what?" Layla questioned.

"He said that if you are not the right Layla you won't be able to see your time-line," said Rasta Rabbit.

"Why does everyone keep questioning rather I'm the right Layla or not? First the rabbits now a gnome!" said Layla.

"Well you've been gone for awhile as you're about to see. Now as you approach the vines they will sense your energy and give way to your time line." instructed Rasta Rabbit.

"The vines will open up as they did before when we first entered?" asked Layla.

"Yes" Rasta Rabbit.

"Okay" Layla answered leaving Rasta Rabbit's side walking towards the vines and Gnome.

"Halt" yelled out Hierba.

"Keep going!" shouted Rasta Rabbit over riding Hierba's instructions while staring him down.

As Layla got closer the leaves, vines, flowers and bushes began to move, Hierba stepped to the side to avoid being knocked down by the moving jungle. As they moved further apart Layla began to see charts filled with numbers and words.

"Awesome!" said Rasta Rabbit over her shoulder approaching her from behind.

"Yeah! Wow!" Was all Layla could accomplish feeling like she was the right Layla indeed, exposing her magic bit by bit!

"Layla, you must build from your past to claim your future! Let's start on the left at our Moon and Earth charts." Rasta Rabbit spoke moving to the left end of the wall.

"Hierba, you are useless and no longer needed." Rasta Rabbit said sharply to Hierba.

Hierba had moved further back towards their right, as not to get swallowed up by the vines. He simply nodded his head and followed Rasta Rabbit's instructions.

"So he does understand English!" Layla said.

"I said that, yeah the evil bastard was just doing his job!" grunted Rasta Rabbit.

"What would he have done if I wasn't the right Layla?" Layla asked.

"He has the power to immobilize you and call the guards, your father's army the Rasta Renegades for any intruders." replied Rasta Rabbit.

"He has the power to freeze Winter?" questioned Layla.

"Yes, as defender of these grounds he holds that supremacy. Winter is aware of this and has *never* set foot on these grounds for that reason," he disclosed.

"Let's turn our attention to the main event!" said Rasta Rabbit, getting them back to the matter at hand.

Layla walked beside Rasta Rabbit, reading the chart, outlined in black chalk on a concrete wall.

"This is kept here to remind us of what we are fighting for...YOU! To get you home and keep you here! To defeat

Winter for all the time she has taken! This chart begins here, when you were exiled by Winter, the year is 1693 on Earth, the Akhet moon cycle on Rastaland you were in your seventh moon cycle or seven years old. As I said our moons have three seasons; Akhet, Peret and Shemu, they each have four cycles and seven fazes as you see on the illustration." Rasta Rabbit explained pointing to each year and moon cycle as he described her life span.

Pointing further down the column he began to simplify her life away from Rastaland.

The full impact of her absence penetrated Layla's being! She couldn't believe someone could hate her so much for nothing! Casting her away as if she *was* nothing!

"You had two lives on Earth that are unknown to us, failed attempts to retrieve you, wasted chances in 1717 and 1741."

"As you've witnessed when viewing your first past life in 1777 our first Earth citing of you. You were born in 1770 in Amsterdam, so you were seven when you were first visited by your parents on the blue planet. Your Rastaland age was ten moons in the second cycle of Shemu," Rasta Rabbit continued.

"We came to seek you four more times; in 1823 when you were in Tanzania, Africa, Winter was powerful. She was in her season of Peret, always consuming magic and purity for the duration of her cycles. As your father stated when he visited, Winter had clogged up every portal making it almost impossible to reach you. Your suffering was felt for realms throughout the universe," a tear formed in Rasta Rabbit's eyes, as he remembered the pain they all felt unable to reach Layla.

"In 1937 in Paris, you were 17 moons in the 2nd cycle of the Peret season, Rastaland cringed as each of your lives grew increasingly complicated. In 1957 in Cuba, you witnessed Winter laughing herself to death after stealing your voice! You were in the first Akhet of your seventeenth moon cycle," said Rasta Rabbit.

As Rasta Rabbit explained, Layla took in the blueprint a lavish sequential of her past.

"To recap," Rasta Rabbit pointed to the top of the diagram, "You were exiled from Rastaland in 1693, lived two uncharted lives in 1717 and 1741, equaling two tries to get you home. Your first Earth citing was 1777, our third try, we visited you the fourth time in 1823 in Africa, a fifth time in 1937 in Paris, and a sixth time in 1957 in Cuba. This seventh and final attempt in two thousand ten. We are in the fourth Akhet, your twentieth moon cycle. What's the next season?" questioned Rasta Rabbit.

"The first season of the moon cycle of Peret! Winter's season!" Layla cried out perfectly comprehending her life graph.

"Yes, and by that time she will know you are here and be in her supreme season! Now each of our moons have seasons, cycles and fazes; as time on your planet has days, weeks and months to measure time. So, you're in our fourth Akhet season, your twentieth cycle and fourth faze. When you complete your final mission, defeating Winter, you will be in the fourth Akhet season, your twenty first cycle and seventh faze. We are in the fourth faze now, in the seventh faze of the fourth season of Akhet a number is added to your moon cycle." elaborated Rasta Rabbit, "When you turn twenty-one you will become the supreme of our realm! We had to bring you back here to aide us in our battle or leave you on earth and lose our minds to Winter. She would rein and rule us mentally and physically eternally, we are immortal!" concluded Rasta Rabbit.

"Well, now that I'm here I'll do whatever I can to help you defeat her!" replied Layla.

The Rasta Rabbit began to levitate again, slowly rising off the ground, moving above her chart.

"And I assure you the more you learn the more confident you'll become! Now off to Ivory Heights we go!" shouted Rasta Rabbit pulling Layla by the hand and into the sky!

Layla found flying exhilarating she held on tightly to Rasta Rabbits paw, soaring above the colorful buildings and beings that was Rastaland. Layla stretched out like super woman and enjoyed the flight. They flew over picturesque views, talking trees and Rasta bees, when the air turned suddenly frigid. Layla noticed the change in climate and snow covered roof tops, she shivered and the Rasta Rabbit hugged her to him warming her with his fur. They glided between the trees a bit before landing with a jump or for the Rasta Rabbit a hop in the snow.

"Do you see the white house?" asked Rasta Rabbit.

"Is it that big white building there with the screaming vines?" answered Layla, describing the vines that made human screams as they rubbed up against one another.

"Well that's a part of it but we're headed to the Ivory Towers that sit in the middle of the white house, it's where the White Witch Winter resides" explained Rasta Rabbit grabbing Layla's hand. The Rasta Rabbit led Layla through a thicket of muddy grass, ice and snow, the haunting path led to the middle of the white house where an open draw bridge awaited them.

"Layla" spoke Rasta Rabbit, "We shall drink this mind reading potion so that no one else can read our minds but each other once we get inside. First you must chant my name seven times in your head before drinking the potion, so only I can read your thoughts. Second, you must think of your favorite song and sing it in your head while drinking the potion. This way only I can read your thoughts and anyone else who tries will only hear the song you thought of. This precaution will protect us from mind control once we enter the Ivory Towers" Rasta Rabbit explained, producing a teeny-weeny bottle from his inside vest pocket offering it to Layla.

"Where's yours?" Layla asked taking the bottle.

"I'm a master of mind read, you're the amateur, drink!" prodded Rasta Rabbit.

"I think I stood on this bottle when I was in your vest pocket earlier." announced Layla examining the bottle and its contents.

"Possibly" Rasta Rabbit stated coolly, holding Layla with a forceful stare, nodding his head towards the bottle implying she needed to drink.

"Will it make me high?" asked Layla.

"Just drink the concoction please." Rasta Rabbit replied.

"What's in it?" Layla asked.

"If it were patience I'd be drinking it! You wouldn't understand the ingredients anyway." Rasta Rabbit replied.

"Try me!" retorted Layla.

"Truth root, mind block salt, reed stop leaf and grey hood juice, hence the color." informed Rasta Rabbit.

"No black girl magic?" laughed Layla.

"Are you going to trust me and drink it so we can move forth or are you going to continue to ask questions and make jokes?" Rasta Rabbit said, his voice held anger but a smile threatened to break through his lips.

"I guess I'll drink it," shrugged Layla as she begins with a dramatic pause twisting the bottle top.

"Chant my name seven times first." reminded Rasta Rabbit.

"Hoot, Hoot, Hoot, Hoot, Hoot, Hoot, Hoot," Layla chants Rasta Rabbit's name in her head.

"Now what song are you going to chose?" asked Rasta

Rabbit.

"Forever Loving Jah by Bob Marley." Layla answered offering her favorite Marley song of praise and protection, she chants the chorus over and over.

Opening the bottle, Layla smelled peppermint, drinking the small dose quickly before she lost her nerve, her tongue went numb as if a minty cough drop was sitting in her mouth after she swallowed. Waiting for the side effects, Layla was shocked she felt nothing and was disappointed it hadn't made her high!

"I feel nothing." Layla said to Rasta Rabbit expressing her views.

"You shouldn't." replied Rasta Rabbit.

"Do I have to continue chanting the chorus in my head?" questioned Layla.

"No, now that you've said my name seven times and chose a song the magic will do its part." replied Rasta Rabbit, "Layla?"

"Yes" answered Layla in her head hearing his voice, being able to communicate this way made Layla feel like her and Rasta Rabbit were one.

"I will speak to you mentally from now until we have completed our mission" Rasta Rabbit continued inside Layla's head.

"Ok" answered Layla in her mind.

"We must shape shift before entering the Ivory Tower" explained Rasta Rabbit "I presume the only way to infiltrate the castle would be to shape shift into one of the Witches Alligator Regulators. As guards, we can effortlessly slip through the cracks! Now to shape shift I need you to think back to the first time you saw the Alligator Regulators and simply envision becoming one! For starters, you can visualize being Mrs. Rasta Rabbit to practice and gain a better idea." finished

Rasta Rabbit

Layla closed her eyes and seeing Rasta Rabbits face in her mind she tried to become him. After what seemed like forever she opened her eyes.

"Am I Mrs. Rasta Rabbit" she asked.

"No, sadly your still lousy Layla!" replied Rasta Rabbit.

"Well I tried!" Layla stated sounding frustrated.

"But do you believe? Do you believe that you can transform into anything you put your mind to! You've shape shifted your entire life from a child to a woman you've worn many masks! I'm just challenging you to tap into your mental instincts! You are holding yourself back! And if it helps, since I know you're a poet at heart, it may be easier for you to say a rhyme in your mind about what you want to be to make it your reality!" tutored Rasta Rabbit.

Once again Layla shut her eye lids and in her head, she said...

"I'm Layla and smoking weed is my habit
when I open my eyes, I'll be Mrs. Rasta Rabbit!"

...Layla opened her eyes.

"Am I Mrs. Rabbit?" she asked Rasta Rabbit.

"Come see!" exclaimed Rasta Rabbit pulling her by the hand to a nearby tree, once they reached the tree Rasta Rabbit said this rhyme...

"I am you and you are me
Dear Brother Tree
allow us to see!"

...a mirror appeared on the trunk of the tree.

Layla could see herself and she was indeed a Rabbit, she had black fur, half rabbit half human, Rasta Rabbits twin.

"Wow!" was all she could manage.

"Okay, now you must become an Alligator Regulator, you must wear the same armor as I do. In Rastaland the Alligator Regulators patrol for all beings, only lions guard Truth's Tower, like those that run the jungle. Our armor distinguishes the Regulators from the Agitatators. So, I'll shape shift first and I need you to mimic what you see so we'll be twins as we are now" Rasta Rabbit explained.

Rasta Rabbit turned his back and Layla observed him mutate from a Rabbit man into a Lizard man. When he turned back around his voice in her head was the only thing she recognized.

"Your turn" he said.

Layla closed her eyes and said in her head..

Lord, its colder out here than a refrigerator
Please turn me into an Alligator Regulator.

"Did it work?" Layla asked Rasta Rabbit in her mind.

"Look for yourself" responded Rasta Rabbit in her head pulling her around so they both faced the mirror tree again. And Layla witnessed the power of her prayers.

"Wow! We both look hungry" Layla said in her head, giggling out loud. It felt strange to feel like yourself but look like a lizard man! But Layla was learning that in Rastaland your imagination was your reality, she found this truly liberating!

"Alright Princesa, being a poet is your power! We will enter the Ivory Towers through the guard's entrance, clock in like we're beginning work and blend in. The Regulators are all followers, so you imitating me won't stand out. Once inside we must locate the regulator Judasemi who will guide us in discovering the Witches weakness, Judasemi knows who you are and is willing to help us. You must remember not to speak with your mouth! We must only and always communicate with our minds. Beware of all and any witches we may encounter and do not drink or eat anything! Keeping your mouth closed and your mind opened is the key to your survival once we enter the Ivory Tower gates!" informed Rasta Rabbit.

CHAPTER SEVEN: I SMELL A WITCH

Advancing upon the Ivory Towers, Rasta Rabbit mentally gave Layla more instructions.

"As I explained before the Alligator Regulators are set apart by their armor. The Regulators that guard our King of course adorn the Rasta colors, red, gold, black and green. The Regulators that guard the White Witch Winter will be clothed in white, their armor glistens at night like diamonds and drip ice during the day. Well, now that our disguises are consummate we shall set our actions in motion. We have one half-moon before the first full moon and fifth faze, we must complete our assignment and exit the Ivory Towers before the Witches clock strikes seven!" explained Rasta Rabbit.

Layla and Rasta Rabbit began their expedition towards the Ivory Towers. Layla had to focus to keep up with Rasta Rabbit. The dynamics of her new physique would take some getting used to. Her feet were wide and flat like a lizard but webbed like a duck, making it easy for her to glide along the ice-covered ground, but if she put her foot down to quick she felt she would tip over. She wasn't accustomed to having such a large nose, it seemed her snout was leading her instead of her legs and she couldn't see that well with her eyes being further apart than usual.

When they reached, the gate leading into the Ivory Towers, Layla realized the entire structure was covered in ice. Layla's upper body being lizard was warm her scales warming her, but her human legs could barely manage the cold.

Rasta Rabbit pressed a button that reminded Layla of a puppy's nose. A buzzer sounded and the gates opened.

Stepping through the gates Layla saw beings that were aliens mixed with evil. Some had faces others were extremely tall some ice skated down the path. Others ate ice cream and snow cones, socializing in a language Layla didn't understand. There were many Alligator Regulators around guarding different entrances. The means of access reminded Layla of an arena, big and spacious with icy walk-ways leading off into other parts of the Tower.

Layla followed Rasta Rabbit who veered to the right once they entered the gates. They reached an opening guarded by a Regulator in white armor who drooled and a witch in all white with a red top hat. The Regulator was digesting something that smelled like spoiled fish, while the witch who had a mole on her nose that seeped out some sort of insect's that crawled out of the mole into her mouth, was throwing a bowl of water into the air watching it turn to snow.

Rasta Rabbit greeted the two.

"Hallo hoe gaat het? We kwamen voor werk, ja? (Hello, how are you? We came for work, yes?)," saluted Rasta Rabbit, to Layla in his head he told her, 'I just greeted them and told them we came to work'.

Layla picked up his thoughts loud and clear in her mind, Rasta Rabbits voice sounded strange when he addressed the Regulator and witch, but in her head, it sounded normal, like her thought with Rasta Rabbits voice attached to it. Layla nodded her head remembering not to speak.

"Goed (*Good*)," responded the Alligator Regulator, his voice sounded like a growl. "We hebben nog steeds werk, kom naar binnen! (*We still have work, come inside*)," he continued.

Layla was getting timorous because she couldn't understand what was said, then came Rasta Rabbits message in her head 'Were in!'

They continued pass the Regulator and the witch, who stepped aside allowing them entry. They arrived at a port that resembled two claws holding hands, unclasping when the gate opened.

The Regulators and Witches were provoking a caged shape shifter, though confined inside a barbed wire barricade, this shifter in a blur of movements transfigured into a lion, owl and a human male in a matter of seconds. Being poked and prodded by his tormentors who yelled verbiage Layla couldn't comprehend. The Regulators and Witches were spitting and foaming at the mouth while hitting the shifter and blocking any attempt of an escape.

As a nervous Layla tread on the heels of Rasta Rabbit she mentally asked him about the caged permutation.

"Who is the trapped shifter?" thought Layla hoping Rasta Rabbit heard her.

"That is Reefa D he is caged here because he defied his people and sold white ice which is an illegal substance here. He was a dealer for the White Witch who caged him here when our courts penalized and ostracized him for his offenses. He placed himself in her hands when he decided to sell white ice" explained Rasta Rabbit.

Layla and Reefa D locked eyes and Layla saw a flash of light in her mind that made her stop walking, but before she could decipher what the mental picture was it disappeared. Opening her eyes Layla almost spoke but before she could Rasta Rabbit who had stopped as well and was now turning back looking at her, he yelled into her mind from his "Silence!"

This interrupted Layla's lips from forming any words, Rasta Rabbit continued speaking with her mentally.

"Don't Speak! Reefa D was trying to speak with you mentally but the Regulators and Witches are so in tuned to his thoughts through their torment they could have read his message, so he stopped. Don't allow your energy or eyes to roam or be read here! We must bypass the check in line and make it to the next inlet and proceed on to meet Judasemi." concluded Rasta Rabbit, as he spoke he pretended to fix Layla's armor. Tapping her shoulder, he spun around and she followed him through the rough crowd of Regulators and Witches.

Most of them were busy agitating the shifter, others mingled about, while some were in the check in line getting their claws scanned before gaining entry. Rasta Rabbit cut straight through the throng of beings, once they passed the line Layla noticed a ledge of clear ice that led to the next opening, it was guarded by one of the ugliest Regulators Layla laid eyes on since being there.

He unlike the rest had white and yellow armor, red veins running through his scales, foam dripping from his mouth and the biggest snout Layla had ever seen. He held a diamond plated machete and of all things his feet were stuffed in ice skates! If Layla wasn't so scared she would have giggled. Instead she stood silent behind Rasta Rabbit.

"Hallo, ik ben Menno, ik ben hier voor Judasemi, alsjeblieft. (*Hello, I am Menno, I am here for Judasemi, please.*)," said Rasta Rabbit.

"Ja, Judasemi wacht op je, een moment. (*Yes, Judasemi is waiting for you, one moment.*)," replied the scary Regulator, turning and skating around the side of the Tower. Layla stole the chance to get an update.

"What's happening?" she thought.

"I told him we were here to see Judasemi and he said that Judasemi was waiting for us and went to get him" answered the Rasta Rabbit into Layla's head picking up her thought.

"He's allowed to leave his post?" Layla thought.

"Oh! This place is heavily guarded, don't look up but sniper Regulators secure the sky!" mentally replied Rasta Rabbit, "Once we greet Judasemi we will follow him inside. Keep up the good work, refrain from speaking and stay on my heels, stepping on them like you have been" continued Rasta Rabbit winking, Layla almost laughed but the scary Regulator was returning with Judasemi in tow.

Judasemi wore glasses that paralleled glass goggles. He was dressed in a white cape with blue moon and star prints, considerably shorter than the scary Regulator, limping, he dragged his left leg behind him.

"Hallo, jongens! (*Hello, guys!*)," Judasemi spoke never making eye contact with Layla; they proceeded around the ice mountain from which Judasemi came.

Walking on the ice path with her lizard webbed feet made it easy. She looked down on the shifter and his tormentors, wishing she could spit on the heads of the Regulators and Witches. It was a short trip around the side and into the Tower. Layla noticed the climate never changed, it was still below freezing!

Once they entered the Tower they entered Judasemi's snow mobile, it was shaped like a white globe with four butterfly doors. Once inside the snow mobile levitated and Judasemi whisked them through the corridors.

On the ride Layla noticed other snow globes commuting to and fro, there was nothing guiding the traffic like lights but everyone seemed to know where they were going and how not to hurt anyone on their way. Below Layla saw all the entrances and citizens congregating, the Regulators and Witches were just as scary above as they were face to face. She felt safe for now, floating in a cave, snow globes entering and exiting all the enclaves.

Judasemi entered a lane that lead deeper into the Tower. He guided his snow globe to the right, riding on a path that had ice ponds on either side. He stopped at an igloo shaped formation and they exited the snow mobile.

They followed Judasemi entering the configuration. The inside took Layla's breath away, all white leather floors, white foam furniture, glass tables, lamps and chairs and above all a fire place! She tip-toed towards the fire, instantly warming her frozen legs.

Judasemi and Rasta Rabbit hugged, Judasemi then left the room going down the hall and came back with two steaming cups.

"Here Layla, you shall enjoy this cinnamon treat, its warm love mixed with cinnamon and melk chocolate." said Judasemi handing Layla a cup.

He handed the other cup to Rasta Rabbit and they all took a seat. Layla melted into the foam chair nearest the fire place. She sipped her drink and was immediately warmed and content. She was so excited to hear her own language, she forgot not to speak!

"Thank you" when the words left her mouth she realized her mistake.

"You would get comfortable and forget all I've taught you" retorted Rasta Rabbit.

"Don't scare her, she'll ruin my floor with chocolate love!" laughed Judasemi.

"Well Princesa you can let your guard down a bit,

Judasemi is on our side!" smiled Rasta Rabbit.

"Yes, I am on your side, the White Witches reign will not last!" answered Judasemi.

"Thank you for helping us and especially for the warmth" smiled Layla.

"Judasemi, we came here to discover the Witches weakness" said Rasta Rabbit getting directly to the point.

"Well our Witch has many weaknesses, one of which is mistreating those of us that serve her. But more than likely you want to own her love stone, her biggest weakness of all! I have it here and you must take it to the Future Forest and warm her cold love stone with your heart, you know for some *love* is a weakness." Judasemi said taking a white pouch from the pocket of his moon and star cape, handing it to Layla. Layla opened the pouch and was blinded by its light. The stone shone like a light bulb, blinded she closed the pouch.

***

Layla squinted from the bright light, she could see a woman she knew was Winter, because a man called her name. Winter was beautiful with wild blond and black Congo dreadlocks, they swung from side to side as Winter shook her head and screamed. The scream resounded in Layla's ears causing her to drop the pouch and hold her hands to her head.

***

Judasemi continued, picking up the pouch and closing the contents inside.

"I guess I should have given instructions first, you must never look directly at the love stone! Once you've reached the Future Forest hold it in your hand over your heart, you must enter the Lake of Life and submerge the stone or you will expose yourself to that dreadful love scene between Winter and her lover Seth. He cheated on her, hardening her cold heart. The scream that froze and shattered Seth and his lover is trapped in the love stone. You hold her heart in this sack! Memories and loves of her past, present and future.

You must know that I created the binding spell for Winter, it was a death spell linked in as well. So, you must kill Winter that is the only way to break the spell, one of you must die! Yet to rectify my ways I am also the wizard that gave Rasta Rabbit his navigating spell to retrieve you." completed Judasemi.

"Why must one of us die?" questioned Layla.

"I placed the essence of both of your beings in the curse, Winter sealed the spell stating that you would have to melt her heart killing her and breaking its hold. She wants to rule your mind and body, dismantling all you love in the process, her hopes were that you would still be on earth instead of here face to face. You are bound by one of the strongest death binding spells in the universe. It's evil I'll admit. One of the counterparts has to die for the curse to expire; the caster or the casted." explained Judasemi.

"And if my family killed Winter, I would have remained on Earth eternally because only Winter or I can break the curse." Layla said to ensure she understood.

"Correct." Judasemi," Your aunt Cleo, overseer of Earth could not break the binding spell and she is guardian of Earth, your brother, one of the supreme sorceress's in the universe could not!" Judasemi shed this bit of knowledge with pride.

"And as I've said, you can't move on with your life until you confront your past. Not being entirely happy on Earth, for example, though you had everything materialistically a person could want. Being reincarnated repeatedly on Earth instead of living your life and ruling Rastaland was what was missing!"

Rasta Rabbit injected into the conversation.

Layla thought about that nagging feeling in her gut, it was there this morning when she woke up. That feeling was guiding her now, telling her that this is real! This is exactly what she had been missing, Rastaland!

"You are our heliacal rising!" smiled Judasemi.

"What's that?" questioned Layla.

"A star rising on an ecliptic path! And I'd love to chat more but now you must hurry, I just received a mental warning that the White Witch has smelled your foreign scent. Though you shaped shifted into a Regulator, the goddess of your essence seeps through your pores. Yet Rasta Rabbit shall get you safely out of the Towers and to the Future Forest!" explained Judasemi.

"Quick!" yelled Rasta Rabbit "You must shape shift from a Regulator into a witch!"

"So I can look like me but wear the white robe and hats as the others?" asked a puzzled Layla.

"Yes, you must change into a white cloth witch!" answered Rasta Rabbit.

"And you must wear this hat that will protect you!" added Judasemi getting up from where he sat moving to a nearby closet where he retrieved a black hat with a wide white brim, the top of the hat was decorated with red moon and stars.

"With this hat they will think you're a sorceress and not trouble! When and if you need to pull the brim of the hat down with a slight tug and you'll be transported to wherever your mind takes you" explained Judasemi placing the hat on his head, he tugged the brim vanishing and reappearing at the door. "You must go now and I'll drink a removing potion that will erase my memory of the last few minutes, so when the White Witch Winter does her mental probing I'll be clear! Isn't that genius! I just created it!" smiled Judasemi

"Bedankt voor alles vriend. (Thanks for everything friend.)," said Rasta Rabbit shaking Judasemi's claws while guiding Layla towards a mirror by the front door.

"Okay Layla its time to show us what you got!" said Rasta Rabbit to Layla.

Layla looked at herself as a Regulator and cringed, she was even beginning to drool like them, being a half lizard half human was not feminine or girly in the least. Layla closed her eyes and became her thoughts, as her mind changed Layla could hear Rasta Rabbit and Judasemi encouraging her.

"Wow!" was all Layla could manage when she opened her eyes.

"Why did you keep changing from yourself into Jessica Rabbit?" questioned a laughing Judasemi.

Layla blushed and the Rasta Rabbit cleared his throat.

"It was one of the first forms I shifted into" explained Layla.

"I thought it was your crush on Hoot" laughed Judasemi.

"Well now that you got it right, we can go!" said Rasta Rabbit ignoring Judasemi.

And get it right she did, Layla thought she made a hot sorceress in her white leather pants suit, she wore a white mink coat and boots remembering the cold and her hat set the ensemble off nicely. She was getting good at shape shifting.

"Once outside we will use the hat to get us to the Future Forest" explained Rasta Rabbit. They both hugged Judasemi and exited his home.

Outside Rasta Rabbit and Layla stood under a beautiful tree covered in snow, its branches protecting them; a snow brella. Rasta Rabbit placed his arm around Layla as she raised her other one to tip the brim of her hat.

In that same instant, she saw her! The White Witch Winter was rounding the corner they came from when they arrived. She had an army of what favored evil looking penguins, they grunted and whistled loudly as all one hundred of them pulled the chariot of ice carrying its platinum dreadlocked counterpart.

Her red eyes bore into Layla's then she yelled her name. Layla's breath caught in her chest! She closed her eyes, which seemed her best defense in this dimension, allowing her full access to her mind, a vital weapon, Layla whispered 'Future Forest' with her soul and prayed for the best!

CHAPTER EIGHT: A WINTER'S TALE

Winter was conceived centuries ago to her parents Boaz and Tapoah, both parents were wizards that taught their children all they knew about magic and how to elevate through dimensions utilizing their minds, her ancestors were sorceress of the elements.

Boaz and Tapoah had three daughters, Cleo seer of earth, Winter of water and wind and the Isis of fire. They resided in a place between Jupiter and Saturn, they existed amongst higher evolved beings that lived to laugh, love and praise the God of all creation.

Boaz and Tapoah taught their children of the purities and malice that is life. Winter was instructed in casting spells, healing beings and creating any world her thoughts could inspire.

Traveling other facets of this mortal coil, spending summers in Pluto, her teenage years partying on Neptune, studying at the University of Superior Sorcery, Winter was groomed to become a prominent well rounded being.

Cleo, her eldest sister was infamous for her guardian work she did on earth and other planets, Cleo utilized her gifts for greatness! An advocate for children and animals alike, she aided rescue workers in forest fires, encouraged single mother's and guarded portals from planet to planet stopping NASA and earthlings from being on the moon. She was now in a war with a gang of aliens from Jupiter who were abducting beings from earth.

And Isis Winter's youngest sister was legendary. In Egyptian mythology she is known as the goddess of nature and magic, protector of the dead. Wife of Osiris, known as the Egyptian God of the afterlife they made quite a pair.

Once they met the true God of life and were appointed King and Queen of Rastaland by their son Ras Fela Winter's hate of her younger sister intensified.

As the middle child Winter, had always felt the need to compete. Cleo had found her purpose in the universe and spent most of her time fleeing back and forth to earth and other dimensions in an effort to keep peace.

And Isis! In Winter's eyes was her parent's prototype! Perfect in her imperfections, everything she touched turned to gold and she herself was fire!

Winter always had a temper and that hot headedness had frozen more than a lover or two. Wind and water being her bending elements by birth, Winter never found an outlet for her passion. She yearned for what her sisters had, a purpose. In her eyes, they were in tune to the vital source initiating their every move. Cleo was in a true battle being a defender of earth and Winter was Isis's battle!

Winter terrorized her baby sister her whole life, casting spells that their mother Tapoah had to tirelessly expel. She was distressed by her daughter's antics, threatening to send her to Saturn's moon Suttung.

Yet not even being sent away to one of the furthest moons could quell her anger. Winter suffered from middle child syndrome, never feeling loved. She felt her parents showered her other sisters with knowledge and devotion. Only noticing the error of her ways and whenever she turned one of her sisters into a frog.

Winter made an attempt to date. Falling in love on one

occasion, Seth has been the only being to melt the harden stone inside Winter's chest.

Winter met Seth at the University of Superior Sorcery, this was also the grounds that fertilized Winter's evil ways. Taught by Professor Jan (pronounced yan) who instructed Winter and her peers in magic, Professor Jan gave lessons in all levels of necromancy, the decorous and the nefarious.

On one occasion while researching 'Tenaus' an insidious type of magic, Winter recognized her desire to be vile, identifying with her lower self, she discovered the negative of a positive and that she was probably named Winter because her heart was ice cold!

During her training Winter was to devise a system that would allow her to travel from portal to planet. Inhaling the 'Tenaus' concoction she could levitate and exist in any realm.

While studying a portal Winter uncovered Steward Suns, a sun being from her dimension 'Lanse' he had been lost for sometime, his family and community had been searching for him for moons. She found him in a portal located near the 'Black Hole' in space. Protected within her 'Tenaus' covering she visited the portal she named 'Land of the Lost' often.

The Land of the Lost was a place of allure and confusion beings from all realms explored this gateway but none stayed. Steward Suns had been trapped there by a binding spell cast by an ex lover, Lana. Winter gathered this information on one of her visits. Never offering her help, never telling anyone that she had found the young native her entire realm was searching for!

Winter was great friends with Lana, the lover of Steward that cast the spell. Winter kept Lana's secret and took great pleasure in the torment of Steward Suns.

Winter had Lana at her beck and call, knowing her secret

gave her power over her as well, while Winter brought Steward food and water from their realm and other necessities in exchange for his sovereignty. Winter drained Steward of his sun fire, collecting it for a rainy day!

When Winter visited, and found Steward dead from lack of nutrients and loss of power, Lana could say nothing about what Winter had done since she felt she placed him there to begin with. Lana never wanted Steward dead, just out of sight, and though she witnessed the evil that resided in Winter, speaking out would also uncover her wrong doing and her father being President of their realm she allowed her fear and status to keep her quiet. In Lana's eyes Steward was a chump who needed to be taught a lesson but she would have snuck him home eventually and he would have lived longer had Winter not stolen his powers.

Winter was empowered by the entire situation she had fire in a jar and the president's daughter under her thumb! Winter didn't see any of the goody two shoes on her level, she despised the truth when lies worked just as well! And she looked forward to her next opportunity to create another victim and she got her chance years later with Layla.

And while she studied more iniquitous theurgy she also conceived love, Seth and Winter took chemispell classes together, Winter knew he was special when she saw his name tag. His was by hers and he hadn't arrived yet. She took her seat and awaited his arrival. And entered Seth Waters, a water bender like her and not only was he an intelligent wizard, topped with flowing locks and looks. He was interested in her!

Their love was written! They attended the same classes, the chemispell teacher sat them by one another and during pot luck they pulled each other's name from the hat!

Winter loved Seth during their season. She planned to be

his wife and mother of his children. For once she set aside her hate of her sisters and focused on her life, wants and needs, no longer an obstacle or targeting those she encountered.

Reality hit when Winter caught Seth cheating in their home, in their bed, under a picture of them together on the wall. After loving him for seven years, she didn't foresee this betrayal.

All Winter could remember after walking in on their moans was her screaming! Locking the scream forever in her love stone, she had to cuff her hands over her mouth to stop. When she opened her eyes everything was frozen. The room, the air, her lover! When she touched him, frozen in his shocked position, he broke into a billion pieces like shattered glass.

After the death of Seth, Winter's rage raised to paramount levels. She had been locked in her arctic home for seven full moons before her family knew what happened. Her father Boaz came to talk to her.

Upon seeing her father, Winter fell into memories of old. How she had always yearned for his full attention and how she never received it until times like now, when she had turned her world upside down and it was too late.

Her parents were consistently a day late and a dollar short of emotions in Winter's sight. When Boaz touched Winter's shoulder, she grabbed his arm and cast a removal spell, hurling him to Triton, the biggest of Neptune's fourteen moons. There she erased his memories and began to fill them with her own.

To this day no one has saw Boaz and though some speculate that Winter played a part in his disappearance, since she was the last being to see him, no one wants to believe a daughter would make their own father vanish!

Yet placing him on the furthest planet from Rastaland assisted in concealing her actions. Neptune having fourteen moons; regular and irregular, she chose Triton because it orbits close to Rastaland during retrograde unlike the outer moons that retrograde orbits far from Neptune.

At the time of Seth's demise Cleo and Isis were prospering, Cleo had successfully redirected a space ship from NASA that was aiming for the galaxy and Isis had just given birth to her daughter Layla.

Winter had all the attention she wanted a moment after her father's disappearance, he was locked away in her special place and her mother enveloped her with love through her grief for her husband.

But when Layla was born, the only grandchild since Cleo and Winter had no children, Tapoah turned her affection towards her granddaughter.

Tapoah missed her husband Boaz immensely, every day she prayed for his return, she saw Layla as a ray of light in her dim universe. Layla became her pride and joy. Tapoah visited Rastaland often to be with her.

To Winter's dismay, Isis was back in the lime light! Everyone she knew was talking about how beautiful the baby was, Rastaland was, Isis was! Winter cringed with envy!

Layla would not only take her mother's place as Queen of Rastaland one day. She would also be groomed to be one of the most powerful enchantresses in the universe! Having the dexterity to shape shift and being educated by Isis and Tapoah, Layla would be unstoppable!

Isis didn't deserve all that authority! Winter should have the husband and rule a place such as Rastaland, birthing the coldest witch in the universe! Cleo could have earth! Rastaland was everywhere Winter wanted to be! And since she was great at making things disappear, why not make Isis vanish too?

Winter started concocting her plan to dominate Rastaland.

Forming an army with Rastaland's weakest links, those willing to follow her lead, Winter explored and percolated the area. Whispering hate me nots into the ears of the beings there, after formulating her gang, Winter targeted Layla.

Gathering like minds was simple it's no trouble finding trouble. Winter began selecting her own Regulators and spawning wicked witches from vile spirits. Winter also familiarized herself with the Ras Text, the Rastaland bible; studying prayers, laws, language, developing her own dialect. Winter abhorred the Egyptian history Ras Fela pulled from Earth placing it in the Ras Text to illustrate his parent's inception.

She had no clue there was a Ras Text that only Osiris, Isis and Ras Fela studied, that held languages and lives that connected them to Layla.

Collecting Layla on the other hand, would take more effort. Layla was safeguarded by her own security which included warrior shape shifters, the Kings Regulators and his army the Rasta Renegades. Patience would be Winter's greatest weapon, and once she saw her opportunity she pounced on it like the soul-eating-witch she is!

She captured Layla wondering away from her labyrinth, after leaving Majesty Hall. Layla had followed a group of Rasta bees to the brink of her destruction. By the time her guards started looking for her; Winter had already taken the seven-year-old Layla to what is now her home, the Ivory Towers.

Once at her home Winter gave Layla a sleeping potion, she then wrapped the child in moss, casting her removal spell, she sent Layla's soul to earth.

Winter knew that her eldest sister Cleo guarded earth and might find Layla, but she could care less because Cleo couldn't break her spell! Winter also knew that Layla missing would expose her scheme.

Beings had been warning Isis about Winter since her arrival in Rastaland. None of that mattered to Winter, once she erased their ability to remember, Layla would become an afterthought of their forgotten thoughts!

When Winter was confronted by Isis and their mother Tapoah about the disappearance of Layla, Winter knew they knew the truth. But it was when Isis asked "Where is my daughter?" that she realized they knew!

Winter knew that Layla and Isis souls were connected, a mother and daughter bond she shared with their mother Tapoah. Isis didn't know where Layla was, but her soul told her Winter did.

Winter attempted to run away from Isis after she asked her where Layla was but Isis caught her with a ball of fire to the back. Winter screamed and turned back to face Isis, using her wind power element to push Isis down as she turned. Isis wasn't down long, jumping to her feet and spraying balls of fire out of wrist like bullets at Winter. Winter blocked the fire using her water power element to extinguish any lingering flames. Winter threw a lamp aiming at Isis but hitting their mother instead! This halted the fight for a second.

"Winter, what have you done?" asked Tapoah in tears. Her tears fell, not from being hit by a lamp, but by the reality of who her daughter had become.

The two sisters stared at each other pausing for their mother's question, then Isis slapped Winter and they begin to fist fight. The entire time Isis was trying to kill Winter blocked all the spells Isis conjured to find her daughter. Winter was looking for the chance to cast her removal spell on Isis!

King Osiris and his guards burst in and begin to separate

the sisters. Once detached, Winter took the opening to vanish, closing her eyes, Winter bolted to the same place she had been staying since entering Rastaland, Pallid.

It is now known as Ivory Heights where she dwells inside Ivory Towers, claiming this section of Rastaland as her own. There she rallied her allies and built a wall on the North side of Rastaland, some say its Winter's icy attitude that changed the once summery atmosphere into Winter Wonderland instead of sunny sweet Rastaland.

Snow begin to fall on the North side of Rastaland the day of Layla's and Winter's exile and snow has fallen only on the North side of Rastaland ever since. Winter's appearance altered as well, her once blond and dark locks turned platinum, her skin albino, her eyes becoming red as fire.

Winter has remained very active in her attempt to overthrow Isis and become ruler of Rastaland, keeping Osiris army out of the territory she stole, keeping Cleo from discovering Layla on earth, trying to kidnap her mother Tapoah, visiting her father in her stash spot, recruiting Rastaland's riff raff and awaiting the moment she will take Isis place as Queen of Rastaland!

Her plot was going as planned until now! What dahell is Layla doing in Ivory Heights? In Rastaland? Outside of Judasemi's house!

They locked eyes and she screamed Layla's name in shock! Then she and that damn rabbit evaporated! Judasemi's name was written all over this oversight! Winter stormed into Judasemi's home unannounced!

"How did she get here and who was that Rabbit she was with?!" demanded Winter.

Judasemi had observed the scene outside and had no time to take his removal potion, besides Layla being outside his door! The jig was up!

"Your parents named you Winter to inscribe your cold existence!" replied Judasemi standing to meet Winter's glare.

"And I should have killed your parents so you'd never be born you imbecile! Now answer my question!" yelled Winter.

"I don't have an answer for your question" answered Judasemi starring down at his shaking hands.

"You helped her!" shouted Winter growing more upset by the moment. "You have betrayed me to the fullest Judasemi! You thought I wouldn't know! That I wouldn't smell that abomination! That I wouldn't trace it back to you! I'll deliver you to the sun!" Winter's red eyes glowed as she focused her hate on Judasemi.

She then took the light out of his eyes, dove into his mind accumulating his thoughts, deciphering confidential components of his psyche.

Winter now knew she was in a war, her opponent already taking the first strike. If she was to win Rastaland the time to act was now!

CHAPTER NINE: THE FUTURE
FOREST

Layla opened her eyes in another place, 'Thank God' she thought, looking into Winter's eyes for that instant gave her a glimpse of what she was up against. Wherever she was now, The Future Forest she assumed was beautiful.

The ground was yellow but you couldn't really distinguish the ground from the white lightening bugs that hovered over everything there was. Layla could see no trees or sky, only lights; moving stars floating by her, in front of her on top of her!

"Are we in The Future Forest?" thought Layla, hoping Rasta Rabbit picked up on her thoughts, not knowing if she could speak or not.

"Si Princesa! This is The Future Forest we are safe here. Now we must locate the Lake of Life so that you can submerge the stone" Rasta Rabbit explained mentally.

He grabbed her hand and they proceeded to walk on the sponge like concrete, the lights in a cluster of profusion moved away from them, on top of them and off again. Once they begin walking deeper into The Future Forest, Layla felt as if she'd sink into the bouncy earth.

The entire amplitude was composed of all of these vacillating luminous creatures. Some were as small as fire flies similar to the ones on earth, others were larger in different odd shapes.

They finally reached the Lake of Life after what seemed like three minutes of walking. The water was apple green and the bottom was illuminated. Layla gazed at the star like beings in amazement.

"Now you must submerge the stone exposing Winter's weakness, liberating her emotions held captive by it. We only have a short time here, you must step into the Lake of Life and warm her love stone of light with your own!" instructed Rasta Rabbit leading Layla to the water's edge.

Layla walked to the middle of the lake, the luke warm water was welcoming, she pulled out the pouch containing the stone. Layla took the stone from the pouch without looking at it, not wanting to be blinded again. She held the stone to her heart, feeling it grow warm beneath her touch, ears roaring from its screams.

The stone became so hot in Layla's hand that she released it. The stone of light began to levitate, flying sporadically in different directions. It boomeranged back and began to hover over Layla.

"Hold out your hand, then submerge it into the lake!" Coached Rasta Rabbit from the side lines.

Layla held out her hands and the stone of light dropped into them. Layla plunged the stone into the Lake of Life in that same moment, the stone of light became warm again, the water bubbling up like a Jacuzzi but Layla didn't let go. Inside her head she heard Rasta Rabbit say "Hold tight! Continue to submerge the stone, you'll know when to let go!" Enlighten the Rasta Rabbit.

Layla started chanting a poem she had memorized back on earth that was suited for the moment:

I be that golden lamb

Created by the great I am
Giving thanks for this universe
My soul the church
Inside we search
For our worth
From the cradle to the hearse
From my mind comes this verse
The last and the first
A queen since birth
Never to be dethroned
Alone nor love stoned!

Her words could be felt in Ivory Heights. Winter had been ransacking Judasemi's home searching for clues as to Layla's whereabouts. When she felt the pull of her love stone! Winter's weakness was love she wanted to be feared not loved. Not only had Layla infiltrated Rastaland and Ivory Heights, now she had her love stone, it could take centuries to retrieve! And without it her harden exterior could be exposed to anything! The last thing Winter wanted to be at a time like this was emotional! She would kill Judasemi again if she could! Layla had to be stopped!

The water began to bubble so hard that Layla feared drowning. Just as she thought to seek Rasta Rabbit for assistance, the stone of light flew out of her hand and into the sky!

Emerging with the other flittering beings, it became one with the light! Layla could no longer decipher it from the others, she turned back walking out of the Lake of Life, hoping the spell was broken. She didn't see Rasta Rabbit, where was he?!

"Rabbit?!" yelled Layla, confident she lost him in all the

light, forgetting out of fear not to speak.

"I'm in your labyrinth Layla" answered Rasta Rabbit in her mind.

"Should I use the hat or my mind to get back?" questioned Layla aloud.

"It's up to you Princesa" responded Rasta Rabbit in her mind.

Layla closed her eyes, now covered with the light beings as all of her was, visualizing her labyrinth, using her mind and the hat, two weapons were better than one! Eyes closed, pretending she was Dorothy in OZ, she was in her own way. Layla tipped her hat instead of clicking her heels. She whispered 'To Layla's Labyrinth' to herself and for the first time felt the shift!

"I felt it!" exclaimed Layla landing two feet away from the waiting Rasta Rabbit.

"You felt what?" asked Rasta Rabbit.

"I felt the pull of gravity shifting me from one place to another, I felt this sort of vibration all over and I knew when I had arrived here!" replied Layla.

"Your beginning to step into your mind literally!" smiled Rasta Rabbit "And you've completed your first task!" He continued excitedly.

"I watched the stone of light merge with the light beings but I don't know if the spell was broken!" explained Layla.

"You broke the spell by getting the love stone of light to The Future Forest. Which is the same forest your brother Ras Fela referred to in your past life. He went there to see when you would return. The Forest is near his palace, he visits often." Rasta Rabbit said informing Layla of one of her brother's favorite places.

"I would love to visit the Future Forest at my leisure as well but, how was getting her love stone of light to The Future

Forest and submerging it into the Lake of Life discovering the White Witch Winter's weakness?" inquired Layla.

"Well, we wanted to weaken Winter's position in the future this is why we took her love stone of light to The Future Forest and not The Past or Present Forest. Having hijacked her love stone has placed Winter in a very vulnerable situation. Someone as perplexing as our witch abhors affection. With her love stone of light apprehended she's an emotional wreck. Used to being in control of her life and others, her heart is now open, she could snap at anytime! It takes a lot of energy and malice to be the wicked White Witch Winter! So with her emotions in a future tail spin, it will be hard for her to focus!" explained Rasta Rabbit, as Layla took this all in the Rabbit continued "Winter knows you're in Rastaland, she killed Judasemi, she knows..."

"She killed Judasemi!?" interrupted Layla.

"Yes, Judasemi and I both knew he would be killed when Winter saw us outside of his house" said Rasta Rabbit.

"Oh! No!" cried Layla.

"No tears Princesa! We celebrate the life of every soul that graduates into the Most High's arms, The Lord has made it so that everything leads back to him, including our spirits, and Judasemi is at peace Princesa. But Winter is searching for you, she knows that you're here, you've Regulated your way into her palace and cast a part of her into the Lake of Life in the Future Forest! I'd say your presence has been felt. Now you must be trained by Ras Fela before you can perfect your next assignment. Defeating Winter's army!" concluded Rasta Rabbit.

"First, back to Judasemi, how do you know he's dead?" questioned Layla.

"Here we can sense or feel for lack of a better term when a

soul has departed this life" answered Rasta Rabbit.

"Wow, well I'mma need a lot of coaching from my big brother!" Layla declared.

"Well you'll have loads of help babe! Starting with what's in your pocket!" proclaimed Rasta Rabbit.

Layla dug into the pocket of her white leather pants suit and pulled out the love stone of light!

"If I cast the love stone of light into the Lake of Life, how is it still in my pocket?" inquired Layla.

"You will need the love stone of light during your final mission it is now in your possession until that time, under your control that's why it's not screaming and blinding you now. Let's not get ahead of ourselves, now that were back in Rastaland we must get going so that Ras Fela and yourself can be properly re-introduced!" explicated Rasta Rabbit clutching Layla's hand he leads the way to Ras Fela.

CHAPTER TEN: TUTELAGE

Over the hills and through the woods Rasta Rabbit and Layla went. She was close enough to scrutinize the patrons she strode past. It was warm in Rastaland and Layla's leather suit was causing her to sweat.

"Can I shape shift into a different outfit?" Layla asked Rasta Rabbit.

"Well be at Ras Fela's palace soon you can change into some training gear then" replied Rasta Rabbit.

"I have to train today?" asked Layla.

"Si Princesa, you only have a short time before completing your second task, so we must fill you up with all the erudition we can muster. You mustn't worry, though Winter has had centuries of practice, kicking her ass will come natural to you!" winked Rasta Rabbit pointing towards the most stunning structure Layla had ever saw.

"We have arrived at the home of Ras Fela, we will enter and your tutelage shall begin." said Rasta Rabbit.

The path leading up to the gate of the palace looked like concrete dreadlocks. The course was suspended over a body of water that surrounded the palace. The bridge they traveled across duplicated dreadlock ropes. The foundation of the fortress was black with seven famous black men carved into the root around in a circle like the black Mt. Rushmore; Marcus Garvey, Malcolm X, Huey Newton, Mandela, Shaka Zulu, Bob Marley and King Osiris finished the cipher. Green topped the black art, illustrating bellowing grass with a face of a being

Layla had never saw before imprinted within. Red was over the green, like a splash of blood against the back drop, displaying an open wound. And the top of the palace was yellow, blending in with the sun, forming a halo over the mansion.

To the right Layla could see a temple made of gold! An angel hovered over the sanctuary, her wings stretching across the sky.

After crossing the dreadlock bridge Layla and Rasta Rabbit was greeted by two black panthers!

"Ras Fela is expecting us" said Rasta Rabbit addressing the panthers.

Before her eyes they both shaped shifted into two human male guards, the one on her left transformed into a tall black man with chiseled features, the panther to her right turned into a guard as equally beautiful as his comrade, though she couldn't gage his ethnicity, each wearing Rasta colored uniforms and armour.

"Welcome Hoot, Princesa" greeted the guard to her left.

Layla smiled as they stepped aside she and Rasta Rabbit entered the palace foyer.

"Ras Fela is waiting for you in his garden" the guard informed them.

"Thank you" replied Rasta Rabbit leading the way towards the light beaming straight ahead, to what Layla assumed led into the garden.

Taking in her surroundings, Layla shadowed Rasta Rabbit, the floor, walls and ceilings were black, green, red and gold like the outside of the palace, reminding her of the room she entered when she first arrived in Rastaland. The décor was solid Rasta colored furniture, every inch of the walls was covered in drawings and art work.

The sunlight, lead them outdoors into a lovely allotment.

Plants, butterflies and the eyes of heaven received Layla.

"I'll step out for a bit so that you and Ras Fela can become reacquainted" announced Rasta Rabbit stepping back inside the door.

"Where is he?" Layla asked looking around seeing no one.

"He will greet you, you must announce yourself!" laughed Rasta Rabbit exiting the garden.

Layla felt alone as soon as he left! He had been at her side since the beginning and she knew he wouldn't bring her this far to desert her!

Layla walked further into the garden, admiring the insects she never saw before and butterflies in colors she could have never imagine.

"Hello!" yelled Layla.

"Hell is low!" came a voice on Layla's right.

"What?" asked Layla.

"I'm over here sister!" the voice.

"Where?" Layla questioned.

"Where do you want me to be?" asked the voice.

"In front of me" asked Layla.

"Okay" the voice.

"Okay, what?" asked Layla.

"Look up!" the voice.

Layla looked up.

"Boo!" spoke a half man, half caterpillar blowing the best smelling herb she ever inhaled into her face, she felt a contact instantly and coughed uncontrollably.

"So our Hoot that you nicknamed Rasta Rabbit chose you?" asked the man a pillar.

"Chose me?" inquired Layla.

"Yes, how can we be sure you're the right Layla?" asked the man a pillar blowing more smoke in Layla's face.

"I am Layla!" said Layla.

"Who are you?" asked the man a pillar very slowly blowing more smoke between each word.

"Layla" exclaimed Layla growing indignant at his accusations.

"Who are you?" The man a pillar asked again with more smoke between each word.

"Can you please stop blowing smoke in my face?" asked Layla fanning and coughing.

Once the smoke cleared she could see him clearly. Sitting on top of the petals of the biggest flower she ever saw, his body was green blending in with the leaves. He had red and yellow veins running through his skin. His face was round, brown and human despite the black antennas sprouting from his locked afro. He had a normal male face, handsome and soft brown eyes, contrasting his harsh voice he was smoking an enormous pipe that looked like it was held up by the smoke it filtered.

"Now we must hone in on your fire ability" said the man a pillar.

"Oh! But you're not sure I'm the right Layla remember!" mocked Layla.

"We'll learn the truth soon enough" said the man a pillar.

"So you're Ras Fela?" questioned Layla.

"Yes, Ras Fela at your service" said Ras Fela blowing more smoke at Layla.

"Why are you a man a pillar?" asked Layla.

"A man a pillar? Umph! I'm a Rasta pillar" explained Ras Fela.

"Why are you a Rasta pillar? I pictured you as you were in King Osiris illustration" said Layla.

"King Osiris is our father little sister and that visual aid was filmed old moons ago, I am a Rasta pillar who will soon morph into a Rasta fly!" clarified Ras Fela.

"King Osiris is my father and you're my brother only if I'm the right Layla" taunted Layla.

"And the Queen Isis would be your mother, so you would've inherited our parent's fire element and shape shifting abilities. You must master both among other things if you are to defeat the White Witch Winter! So as I've said now we must sharpen your fire element capabilities" explained Ras Fela.

"Fuego! Vuur! Fire!" Ras Fela yelled startling Layla.

She observed the atmosphere shift around her. The garden was transformed into a gymnasium.

"Are we in my high school gym?" asked Layla bending down to touch the waxed basket ball court that once was plants and dirt.

"If you recognize where you are, you may be my sister after all!" observed Ras Fela.

Upon hearing his voice, Layla turned to see that Ras Fela had transformed as well. He was the tall, dark, regal black man that she saw in the portrait of him in King Osiris illustration. His long locks touched the floor as did his beard, he resembled a black Moses!

"I have waited one hundred and sixty years for this moment!" Ras Fela walked to Layla taking her into his arms. He smelled of coconuts and Kush oil, his locks smelled of almonds. She felt safe in his arms and she could feel by his grip that he missed her a lot. Stepping back, he pushed her away and looked her up and down.

"We will never lose you again!" Ras Fela stated, his eyes confirming his seriousness.

"Are you Bob Marley reincarnated?" Layla asked.

"No." laughed Ras Fela, "Why'd you ask that? Because of all the Rasa colors?" Ras Fela asked.

"That and the name *Rastaland*." replied Layla.

"I am a being created by the Great I Am! An extension of God's image, known as Horus in Egyptian mythology, Panton in Pluto, Ze Ze in the realm of Revelation and a child of God in the realm of the absolute, where we all return, review and begin again! I am fire, flesh, shape shifter, put all together I am a son of God, a being of light. I love those colors; red, black, gold, green; blood, beings, sun, earth. Here you are reminded by the colors of life everywhere you look!" explained Ras Fela.

"Were you a Rasta in another life?" asked Layla.

"Well, Ras Tafari the tittle Ras and the first name Tafari Makonnen comes from who?" Ras Fela said, answering Layla with a question of his own.

"Halie Selassie I "answered Layla.

"Ras means?" Ras Fela asked.

"Head." answered Layla.

"Yes, an Ethiopian title equivalent to Prince." continued Ras Fela with the rest of the definition.

"And Tafari is equal to Jah or Jehovah, I asked a question first. And I'm well informed and in tuned to Rasta culture, Bob Marley taught me it was okay to be black." Layla said.

"How do you mean?" asked Ras Fela.

"Well my world was completely white before he entered! My God, my thoughts, the person in my head that I wanted to become! Mr. Marley reached up from the grave and touched me! Showed me that being who I am was perfect, big lips, hips, nappy hair and all! At sixteen, when I discovered his music, I was introduced to another way of life!" elaborated Layla.

"We are all Rasta's in our hearts, rather we acknowledge it or not! We are all God's!" Ras Fela's skin glowed as he continued, "Recreating, remembering, recovering ourselves through Thee Creator! Rastaland was formed light moons before the ideology of the Rastafari movement that arose in the nineteen thirties on Earth. I'm a Rasta man in my heart 'alles or always', Princesa, to answer your question. Bob Marley was a phenomenal man of Jah. Thee Creator with a guitar, his connection with the God of his ova standing is so close that his music still resonates decades after his death. Teaching and strengthening generations of the past, present and future. I love Mr. Marley as well, but let me assure you, I am not Bob Marley nor Hallie Selassie I. I am your loyal brother, friend and soon to be trainer!" exclaimed Ras Fela.

"Yes, Rasta Rabbit told me I was to train today." replied Layla.

"Si, and we will begin here with this obstacle course you see before you." said Ras Fela.

Layla had noticed the balance beam and yellow and green striped cones, when the scenery changed from the garden to the gymnasium.

"Our first lesson is in fire!" Ras Fela walked until he was face to face with Layla ,"I wish we could relax and relish in your return, but we have a deadline to make before we play catch up." Ras Fela hugged Layla tightly to him once more.

"You are my savvy, super, supreme sistah! And I love you more than words can express. I've missed you more than the harvest could ever miss the rain! Once you've vanquished our Winter affair we can re-establish our relationship, now I'm ecstatic you're here and I must prepare you for what you're up against!" reflected Ras Fela.

"Why is Winter so hateful towards me? Accomplishing all she has? All she desires to do?" questioned Layla.

"Winter's hate is really her awe of you! Her love for our mother twisted into fear, manifested as evil deeds. You must not ponder past actions, your review of your past lives illustrated we were with you the entire time, did they not?" asked Ras Fela.

"Yes they did." replied Layla.

"That's all that matters! She has already failed! Winter has no clue we visited you on Earth, that we created a language of our own dedicated to you in our bible, Ras Text. Her threat of causing us to forget you only made us search harder! And now you're here!"

"You're right! I'm here and that is all that matters! Let's get too it!" shouted Layla, now excited for the training ahead.

"Yes! Winter is aware of your presence here in Rastaland and we are now in the fifth faze of our moon cycle, still in the fourth season of Akhet. Did you fully comprehend the chart?" asked Ras Fela before he continued.

"You are doing a great job little sister! Since you've been in your labyrinth and conquered your first mission, recouping Winter's love stone, the moon has moved a faze, we have two more fazes before your moon day! Or Earth day." Explained Ras Fela.

"You mean my birthday?" asked Layla.

"That's what I said." replied Ras Fela.

"Well you were close." giggled Layla.

"Let's begin with fire, shall we?" answered Ras Fela, smiling, pointing to the balance beam that stood in the middle of the gym.

Layla and Ras Fela walked to the balance beam, taking Ras Fela's hand, Layla mounted the beam. Balancing herself on the ledge Layla put one foot in front of the other. Once stabilized, she let go of Ras Fela's hand and awaited instructions.

He pointed upward toward seven gold hoops that hung from the ceiling.

"You must aim your fire towards the hoops" explained Ras

Fela

"How? I've shape shifted before but I've never thrown fire!" Layla announced growing sweaty with the thought of her task.

"Push the fire out from your soul! As part sun being your soul is eternally ignited!" instructed Ras Fela flicking his wrist and throwing out a ball of fire through the hoop above Layla's head.

Layla ducked though the ball of fire came nowhere near her, almost toppling off the beam.

"Seriously! How can I keep my balance and duck at the same time? I'm too nervous to get in touch with my soul with you throwing fire at me!" Layla snapped attempting to get down off the ledge, but before she could put her foot down, the waxy gymnasium floor turned into muddy quick sand in front of her eyes. Layla looked at Ras Fela, her eyes as big as marbles.

"What's happening?" Layla screamed.

"You can't dismount! You must summon the fire that lays dormant in your soul!" Ras Fela explained safely from his spot in the gym, the place he stood was still hardwood floor.

"What happened to the nice brother that missed me so much? Why would you turn the floor into mud?" asked Layla indignantly.

"I'm still your sweet brother, yet you just expressed you are aware of our deadline, did you not?" questioned Ras Fela

"Yes, but" Layla squealed mustering all the self restraint she had to stop herself from falling into the quicksand that was beginning to bubble.

Ras Fela cut Layla off before she could continue.

"We don't have time! What I am asking of you is already inside of you! You must pull the fire out of you! Like you pulled the shape shifter out! We don't have the time for you to catch on! Only you can lose yourself and free your mind! And fire will be one of your greatest weapons in conquering Winter. Winter is of the air and water elements; with water, she makes ice and we all know fire melts ice! So, I need you to stop pretending your pretending that you're pretending and let's pretend you really are the Princesa of Rastaland, my sister, who can melt those rings of ice with the fire in her soul!" shrieked Ras Fela.

Layla looked at the once gold rings that were now dripping water, the atmosphere had changed from the gymnasium to Winter Wonderland, the hoops suspended in mid air, the ground bubbling with mud and Layla hadn't even noticed the rings and wind…until now!

"Well, when I shape shift I rhyme to aid the transition, do you have any tips I could use for throwing fire from my wrist?" ridiculed Layla stretching her arms out in front of her to stabilize herself.

"Layla, the reason I can turn the floor to quicksand and the atmosphere to ice is because I believe I can! Every moment of your life you create!" replied Ras Fela.

"So I created the situation between Winter and I?" asked Layla.

"To some degree, you did run away from your labyrinth that day that Winter captured you. You were seven, old enough to listen and act accordingly. We told you on numerous occasion's Winter was not safe and not to be out alone, how she and her goons lived amongst us, but you were stubborn then, just as you are now." replied Ras Fela.

Layla could since the truth in her brother's words, she was still that tenacious little girl in the inside, even if she couldn't remember the moment he described.

"Well that maybe true but that was not a suggestion." Layla stated looking down at her wobbling feet, looking back very slowly at Ras Fela who stood at ease, arms crossed.

"You must control your thoughts and focus. I bet your mind is shaking as you are now." Ras Fela said, slyly commenting on how Layla had begin to shake because of the cold.

"Help me…brother" Layla paused before saying brother, a plea for physical assistance.

"You don't believe anything I'm telling you!" observed Ras Fela.

"Would you?" yelled Layla "If someone took you from everything you knew and showed you things you could never imagine!" explained Layla growing discouraged.

"You're blessed Layla! But you can only help us if you believe! You have to believe in your abilities to master Winter!" informed Ras Fela.

"I'm cold!" yelled Layla forgetting their conversation momentarily as what paralleled an arctic Chicago breeze blowing through her coat. She was happy she hadn't changed after all!

"Build a fire!" said Ras Fela sarcastically.

Layla screamed out of pure aggravation, she was freezing! It seemed the temperature was dropping by the second.

"It feels like it's getting colder!" said an observant Layla.

"It is!" Ras Fela answered sitting snuggly in only the black pants suit he wore, a black, green, red and gold cape and boots completed his ensemble.

"Why aren't you cold?" Layla asked Ras Fela shivering.

"I'm warm inwardly!" laughed Ras Fela. "I will give you a tip before you freeze to death! Utilize your mind, picture warmth, remember what it felt like when you accidently burned yourself, visualize the sun, pull the hottest day you can imagine from your fingertips" said Ras Fela feeling empathy for the freezing girl, he continued, "I was blessed with this realm because of my strong faith and belief! I know God's promise is real and everything I imagine I can experience! Because that's what we are, living and breathing beings, God in the physical! God's imagination illustrated through our actions." concluded Ras Fela.

"We are God's?" asked Layla.

"You said it! Now believe it! Dig deep and become the Goddess you know you were born to be!" Ras Fela coached the strength he felt building within her.

"All I can think about is how cold I am and I don't know how long I can stay on this balance beam!" Layla yelped.

She could only wrap her arms around herself in increments because she had to constantly stick them out to prevent from falling.

So she wrapped her arms around herself briefly to protect her body from the gust of wind. She couldn't identify the terrain but she sensed frost bite would set in soon!

"Oh!" yelled Ras Fela over the wind, "Getting angry might help you catch a fire!" he informed.

Now Layla was freezing mad! She closed her eyes and visualized the opposite of her experience, sun, warmth, clear skies. Still she felt wind, cold and was that rain!? Layla opened her eyes.

"Nope, not this time kiddo! You must learn to see with your mind, eyes wide shut and focused!" coached Ras Fela.

"What a bad teacher you are! The child will congeal before she catches fire!"

Layla turned in the direction of the strong feminine voice, Queen Isis stood across from Ras Fela.

"Sunshine!" commanded Queen Isis

And the ambience fluctuated into a 70 degree spring slash summer period, Layla stood in awe and relief, the cold, balance beam and mud vanished!

"Welcome home baby!" said the Isis of fire walking towards Layla, placing her hands on either side of Layla's head. Layla was instantly jolted into Isis' memory of fire through her touch.

***

They were in a field of dandelions and tulips; they were walking fast over the enclosure. The Isis of fire looked as Layla remembered, but she was a little girl.

"Use the fire inside of you if you need to!" Isis of fire said us they trotted faster and faster, Layla felt like running, felt like something was chasing them.

"Is someone chasing us?" Layla said in her head, but her mouth said "Is iemand ons achterna?"

"Si, Princesa, estás en peligro! (Yes, Princesa, you are in danger!)," replied Isis.

And then Layla saw her! Winter was advancing on them swiftly army in tow. Layla sprang into action, flicking fire from her wrist she caused the field in front of them to catch a blaze forming a circle of fiery protection, halting Winter, they took to the sun!

***

"I remember that!" shouted an excited Layla.

"Si, Princesa, you were six and we were practicing defense mechanisms, I would create scenarios for you to think your way out of. I guess a mother can never prepare her child for everything" sadly explained Isis. Layla looked at this beautiful glowing woman! Her skin glowed, complimented by her blond shoulder length locks and petite frame. She looked liked the Goddess she was in her yellow jump suit and Rasta colored boots.

Layla would be honored to call this woman mother! Isis continued "I taught you the Rasta colors, black for the beings that prosper, green for the land that's thriving, red for the blood that pumps through our veins, yellow for the souls of sun, I educated you on fire power and shape shifting forms, on our language, as your mother. Thee Creator blessed me as your teacher! And those freckles on both of your hands, your birthmark; or as we refer to them here 'soul marks', prove to me you're my daughter! During your exile on earth you've had those marks on both hands in every life! They shine now because you are beginning to believe." concluded Isis.

Layla looked at the backs of both her hands, the freckles on her hands sparkled! Remembering her past life in Cuba, in her heart she felt the connection and smiled.

"I saw you in Cuba with me! You gave me back my voice, and memory by touching me then as well!" recounted Layla.

"Yes, that was a close call Princesa! We had to succeed this time! Winter was a moment away from discovering my visit to Earth! We did all we could! And now our love and perseverance has paid off! You're home! I'm never letting you go!" Isis hugged Layla, crushing her against her chest. Isis smelled of Egyptian musk, of course she would, Layla thought to herself.

Ras Fela walked over and placed his arms around his mother and sister protectively.

"The time has come to place this love into defending our lives!" Ras Fela commanded towering above the women he loved, ready to get down to business.

"Yes, let's begin! I've waited for a long time for your return, now that you're here we will set aside a time frame to bridge our alliance, but for now let the drills begin!" the Isis of fire roared.

CHAPTER ELEVEN: A SUMMERIZATION OF LAYLA'S TUTELAGE

During Layla's preparation, Isis instructed her to put Judasemi's magical gift to use. Layla was shown by Isis how to pull strength and direction from her spell binding head piece, while exercising her fire techniques, Layla turned to her hat to aid her in tuning into her fire element abilities.

Tipping her bonnet Layla could feel the fire racing through her blood. It reminded her of how she felt when she ran in the afternoon, in July, when the sun was at its hottest, the combination of running and the heat made her feel like she would spontaneously combust!

But instead of wanting an air-conditioned room, Layla craved to release the fire. The built up pressure forced her arms to stretch upward, palms up and out, it felt like the heat from her body and blood became a ball of power forcing itself out of her wrist.

Layla shot two balls of fire, one from each wrist into the sky! She was so thrilled she screamed and ran to Isis, jumping into her arms!

"Now that you know who you are and you are familiar with the elements of life, life's intensity, life's fire, detonating from your soul, you must remove your crutch and aim from yourself" advised Isis in Layla's ear during their embrace.

Layla stepped out of Isis' arms and into her own mind.

Removing her hat, she recited the word 'fire' in her head until she again felt the pulsating heat seeping through her pores.

"Where are the hoops?" Layla asked Ras Fela, the frozen rings and balance beam had vanished when Isis change the atmosphere.

"All around you" replied Ras Fela raising his right arm, pointing in the air he turned in a circle seven gold rings appeared in each place he pointed, a balance beam made of gold, chained by diamond links to a tree, stood in the middle of the grassy field they were in.

Layla mounted the beam and opened fire literally, aiming at the gold hoops, some of her balls of fire made their mark, others missed the rings completely, and some caused Isis and Ras Fela to duck! Layla was swiftly studying and retaining her fire element techniques, running up and down the ledge shooting fire from her soul. After she had enough practice aiming at the hoops, It was time to learn how to become the fire she released.

Isis put into words Layla's mission, "Sometimes you will have to become fire for protection, other times you may use your element as a weapon and blow things up!" explained Isis guiding Layla by the hand and climbed the steps of the sun. Isis continued, "You are a sun soul being, the fire inside you never dies and will guide and protect you eternally, the more you practice the more you will be able to channel your spiritual inferno" concluded Isis sharing a glimpse of the sun soul existence with Layla.

***

Layla was devoured by the flood lights of the sunrise, too much for her eye sockets to consume, Isis shielded her eyes with her hands, Layla saw the sun beings who sat in a circle around the sun absorbing its power, she was warmed by the sun's embrace.

As they walked the stairs of sun, Layla held her mother's hand tightly, remembering her past life in Cuba with Isis, Layla recalled a special moment they shared.

"I yearned to be here when I was in Cuba, desired to learn my place in the sun." Layla initiated the recollection, "Now I'm here!" Layla whispered through her smile.

She felt amazing! Warmed by the sun of life, the fire that coursed through her veins made love to the suns heat, making her head heavy, her body sweaty and her soul rejoices! "Yes love" smiled Isis, "As I told you then, our love for you is the remedy!" Replied Isis, waving her hand in front of them...

***

They were back in the grassy field with Ras Fela.

During the next moon Layla studied her element fire, Isis was head coach but Ras Fela and the Rasta Rabbit chipped in to bring her lessons learned to life.

Layla mastered fire balling, got good in staring at things until they blew up! She would see the explosion in her mind first and create it in her reality. It took a lot of concentration, look out Drew Barrymore, Rastaland's true fire starter was about to make her mark!

Layla also adapted procedures to aide her in her shape shifting proficiency. She was educated by Ras Fela on how to remain in her shape shifter form no matter the threats, Ras Fela coached Layla in transforming from one image to another and how to become multiple shapes at one time. This lesson was to ensure that Layla would never revert to herself if she becomes frightened during a confrontation.

Layla enjoyed herself as she became more comfortable in who she was, what she is and what she is capable of and how to complete her mission.

After Isis and Ras Fela felt Layla was up to date in her fire element and shape shifting skills they upped the training to physical combat!

Layla, after absorbing so much so fast was now going to be tested in a duel style conflict, Rasta Rabbit her willing opponent. There were three rounds to be fought, the first that defeated their rival two of the three rounds won. Each cycle would have something to do with what Layla learned, fire element, shape shifting and mortal combat. Before the match could begin, Layla raised her hand and spoke up!

"Ummm…ahem…All this is new to me and no one said anything about mortal combat!" stated a nervous Layla.

"Just flow with what you know, stay in tuned to your glow and don't be so serious it's just a show!" rhymed Ras Fela escorting Layla into the ring, winking as he spoke.

"Come on Layla, show me what you got!" taunted Rasta Rabbit.

The first-round Layla impressed herself, ducking Rasta Rabbits carrots juice pellets with her soul fire, she thought of it as a fiery ping pong game! Blocking the carrot bullets with fire from her palms, firing back whenever she could, Layla became very flexible, astonishing herself with her back-bending skills.

Layla won round one by catching Rasta Rabbit in the face with an unexpected fire ball to his right eye socket. As Rasta Rabbit shook off the pain in his corner, Layla couldn't help wondering if he'd let her win.

Ras Fela sounded the bell and the gathering of about three hundred on lookers began applauding, Rasta Rabbit was cute in his Rasta colored boxing shorts and Layla looked nice and fit in her red jumpsuit and kicks!

Ras Fela stepped into the middle of the ring and addressed Layla, Rasta Rabbit and growing crowd,

"Congratulations on round one Layla, round two will target shape shifting, Isis will call out a name of an animal, being or phase and you two must become that image through shape shifting. If Layla wins this round she is the winner, having won the last round as well!" Ras Fela concluded exiting the ring after Layla and Rasta Rabbit touched gloves.

Layla knew whoever won two of the three rounds was the winner, she figured Rasta Rabbit let her have round one but now she'd have to work harder for a victory.

Isis clapped her hands three times and began the contest,

"Kikker, Rana, Frog!" shouted Isis.

Rasta Rabbit became a green frog, complete with his lily pad he stuck out his tongue and snapped a frozen Layla on the leg with it!

Snapping out of it, Layla became a toad and jumped onto his back! Layla was becoming stronger in her beliefs of Rastaland and all she had encountered. Observing Isis, Layla wanted to mimic her every move, proud to be a soul sun being!

"Tiger!" commanded Isis.

The Rasta Rabbit became a Bengal tiger and Layla his tigress!

"Uil, Biho, Owl!" Isis yelled.

The Rasta Rabbit and Layla took to the sky, the crowd along with Isis and Ras Fela cheered as the two soared above their heads.

Layla was learning that when you took form of whatever you shape shifted into you become that image, the instincts of that being taking over your own. So now she was literally an owl, following Rasta Rabbit above and beyond, Rasta Rabbit turned sharply to the right and circled back around Layla, he shot balls of carrot juice at her, startling Layla who was just getting comfortable flying!

"Stay in your shape shifting form and defend yourself!" coached Rasta Rabbit.

Layla thought he wouldn't help her since he was her opponent, but this mock battle was set up to train her. Coming out of her head, Layla begin flying higher and lower dodging the Rasta Rabbits carrot bullets.

"Try to shoot fire in your shape shifting form!" instructed the Rasta Rabbit.

Layla flew fast through the sky with Rasta Rabbit trailing her. Flying came natural to Layla in her owl form, as she flew she looked back and fired at Rasta Rabbit through her wing. Layla and Rasta Rabbit knew that Layla was prepared, that she was ready that she believed!

After ascending the Rastaland skies Layla and Rasta Rabbit returned to the ring where the match was held. They landed as owls, Rasta Rabbit shape shifted back into himself, he wore a gold cape and black pantsuit and jacket instead of his usual Rasta colored get up. Layla transformed into herself wearing her red jumpsuit she wore prior to their competition.

The crowd quieted down as Ras Fela stepped into the ring and began to converse with Layla and the audience.

"Our Princesa and always our winner. Layla, you have come into your true self here in Rastaland, and with the help of our mother Isis, myself and new found friend Rasta Rabbit. I've watched you blossom in the short time of your tutelage. Now, all of Rastaland will fast and pray before taking our next step, defeating the White Witch Winter. During our fast we shall refrain from communicating, we shall sacrifice seven lambs of life and we shall offer our souls in prayer. May the Most High hear our hearts, moving swiftly before us, for the victory is the Lord's!" Nema everyone responded in unison, vanishing and reappearing at the temple, except Ras Fela, Layla and Rasta Rabbit.

"Why does everyone disappear when they say the word…" Layla was cut off by Isis before she could finish.

"Nema" Isis completed her sentence.

"Yes" Layla replied.

"Nema is a very magical word here in Rastaland. It is Amen backwards. We use Nema as you do there to end prayer. You will also be transported to where ever your thoughts take you." explained Isis.

"Like you did in Cuba and my father did in Africa during my past lives?" questioned Layla.

"Yes, exactly, we were caught up in the rapture of our prayers and transported home." replied Isis.

"What is Rastaland like?" asked Layla taking Isis's hand and strolling away from the ring in the direction of the Golden Temple.

"You mean how is it living here?" Isis inquired to be sure she understood her daughter's question correctly. Enjoying the walk and talk with her beloved.

"Yes, how are the beings here? Where do they work? Do you have currency?" Layla asked.

"The beings here are soaring spirits or HEB'S; Higher Evolved Beings. Planet Earth is very primitive; Thee Creator has given them the clues and tools but they choose as individuals to live in anxiety and stress! How humans love drama! They love it! Bless them! Here the creatures do jobs that they love for the community, the elders raise the children, we don't have money we have magic, we exchange deeds, build our realities with our imaginations! Everyday here is paradise a true utopian life." answered Isis.

"We do jobs from our soul." chimed in Ras Fela walking up alongside Isis and Layla.

"Describe a day in the life of people in Rastaland for me?" asked Layla.

"Well," began Ras Fela smiling at his mother Isis who chuckled, "You would wake up, give praise for that day and smoke God in his weed form; a joint packed with the greatest cheeba! Then you would bath in the spa of liquid life, after getting dressed you would bike, fly or think your way to Lyrical Libations, our library, since you're a poet at heart, you would get there right before lunch!" Isis burst into laughter, Layla smiled and Ras Fela continued, "And say a poem blessing the food and you would eat fish and onions, peppers and garlic with some Rasta stewlu and vegetables, washing it down with Jaga Juice, it tastes like...strawberries?

Then you would bike to the Golden Temple for daily prayer with all the citizens of Rastaland, to burn off your meal. Then off to the Tree Park to dance to the drums and around the fire, meeting your friends there you would go to Lava Lift afterwards, Rastalands amusement park and ride the tallest and biggest creatures in our realm.

After that excitement you'd stop at the community center before going home to check in and see if your assistance was needed with cooking, helping an elder being, inspecting the growth of our fields or examining a soul being on the sun. Then you would leave the center, go home and have dinner with your family. Give praise, smoke more ganja and pass out! This is an everyday example of an adult's life here, you may study, time travel in the Future Forest, there are numerous options to choose from. As Princesa, you would run the City of

Osiris, amoungst other things." Ras Fela summarized.

"So the community center let's you know what needs to be done?" asked Laya.

"We govern ourselves here, we know what needs to be done and we get it done! If you are good with plants you would assist with growing our food and maintaining our gardens. If you're a great instructor you teach, if you're a poet or musician you entertain, you do what you feel. Your emotions guiding you along your path." Ras Fela replied.

"A lot of praying and smoking going on!" laughed Layla, they all laugh at Layla's observation.

"What's so funny?" asked Osiris appearing from thin air, He was seven foot seven inches tall, three inches taller than Ras Fela, his aura penetrated their conversation. His eyes were hazel, his long dreadlocks shifting in the wind, the Rasta charm around his neck hypnotized Layla.

"Your daughter is quite the charmer." smiled Isis.

Layla and Osiris locked eyes, Layla ceased walking, looking up at her father, she could see his resilience and resolve, this man loved her, his eyes spoke his heart.

"I'm sure she is." Osiris said smiling down on Layla.

"I'm blessed that you are home and proud you are beginning to believe." Osiris said to Layla taking her by the hand, the family resumed their walk to the Temple.

All the citizens of Rastaland were dressed in gold as they formed a line, moving towards the Golden Temple guarded by the hovering angel Layla saw upon arriving at Ras Fela's palace. Layla followed behind Ras Fela, Isis at her left, King Osiris at her right, and the Rasta Rabbit behind her.

Everyone entered the Golden Temple of praise saluting the Most High and kneeling humbly in prayer. The guardian angel above the Golden Temple greeted Layla with a nod. The angel was gold like the Temple her wide wings casting shade over the haven, her eyes were white clouds and her golden locks blew in the Rastaland breeze. She blew ganja smoke over Layla after nodding Layla was embraced by her love cloud of sistah smoke. When the fog cleared, she was in the foyer of the Temple.

It was a breath-taking sight to Layla; The Temple was gold as was the ground, gates, windows and everything inside. The pews were set in a circle, a small platform was in the middle of the wide circle of golden pews, the ceiling and walls were gold with white wings like angels peaking out through the walls.

Rasta Rabbit gave her a slight tug and escorted her to the nearest bench, Layla realized as she walked that she was wearing a sequence gown made of gold chips, the top of the gown wrapped around her neck like a flower it was pure elegance with golden slippers to match. They kneeled on the padded golden pillows that sat under each bench for that purpose.

A bell rang seven times and every being in Rastaland kneeled in prayer to Thee Creator!

CHAPTER TWELVE: WAR

The fast lasted for one full moon in Rastaland time, for Layla or earthlings it would have felt like a month, to Layla in the Temple it felt like hours of pure bliss.

Layla was brought up spiritually and introduced to God at a young age on earth in this life time; she knew God created the universe and every dimension in it! So, where ever Layla was she knew Thee Creator was with her! She felt that all things lead back to God, as would this experience. So, fasting; spiritually tuning in and channeling your energy to the Most High came natural to Layla.

Layla fell into a deep meditation as did the other beings of Rastaland; it felt like falling from one dream world to the next. She began her prayer thanking Thee Creator for keeping her safe for guiding and protecting her. She was honest with God her friend, she explained how she really didn't understand what was happening to her but felt it was bigger than her! That this was her calling what she was born to do. She prayed for guidance and protection for God to guide her to his will, may God's will be done was Layla's prayer. Layla knew no matter the outcome of the battle, Thee Creator was in control! And this journey was teaching her NOT to question everything! She wouldn't have made it this far if she'd questioned every step.

Layla was encircled by Rasta Rabbit, Ras Fela, Queen Isis of fire and King Osiris. Osiris handed Layla a scroll, Layla unrolled the scroll and realized it was blank.

"It needs your breath of life." Osiris instructed Layla who

stared at him blankly.

"Blow onto the scroll, lady." prodded Osiris.

Layla did as she was instructed, the scroll revealed the prayer of Rastaland that all citizens recite from heart to signal the end of prayer;

Kings and Queens shall come forth out of Rastaland and stretch forth our hands before Jah. Thou Lord of Thy Divine Majesty, We exalt your eternal breath. Thy immortal spirit dwells in our hearts, we are your paths of righteousness. Your great expression manifested, rule I and I, may your will be done, may your unconditional love and mercy bind us in forgiveness of ourselves and one another.

We honor your wisdom, paying homage to the present that is a gift, our souls nourished, the sick cured, our beings protected. Deliver I and I from the hands of our enemy, that I and I may prove fruitful in these vexing times. Our adversaries have passed and decayed in the depths of you, to be reborn anew. O how we glorify thee for our place in thy kingdom forever and ever. We hail our Majesty Thee Creator God, great and powerful God, Jah, who sitteth and reigneth in the heart of beings. Heed us, anoint us and bless us as we pray your loving face radiates with joy because of us. We pray you continue to bestow your blessings upon our realm, guide and protect us eternally Thee Creator we pray. Nema.

The beings all vanished after their prayer, including Layla, after reading the prayer and saying Nema, she found herself in the Rasta skies floating above the Temple.

Layla was embraced by her parents as they glided along

the shores of Rastaland. Isis took the time to educate her daughter on what was to come.

"Layla darling" began Isis "We are in a fight for our minds! The Rasta Renegades were sent away before us and put in place for battle. While we were praying, Winter was waging war! Setting traps, yet Jah will only allow her to go so far! We must commence and plunge right into action now that our fast has ended. It is time my child. Time for you to do exactly what you came here to be!" concluded Isis.

Layla blinked and realized she was suspended in mid air over a football field of Rasta colored tulips.

They arrived in what Layla assumed was a garden in Truth's Tower but she asked Rasta Rabbit to be sure.

"Are we in Truth's Tower?" Layla asked Rasta Rabbit.

"Si Princesa, we are on Truth's Tower lawn, King Osiris and Queen Isis' palace, your labyrinth is adjacent," replied Rasta Rabbit.

"Layla" King Osiris spoke to Layla, the four of them hovering over the garden in a circle, sitting Indian-style mid air. "Layla," King Osiris continued saying her name twice over the commotion overhead, "We are in the mist of combat! The Rasta Renegades are moving in surrounding and striking Winter's army with a surprise attack. I also have allies with other planets and dimensions supporting my efforts to subdue Winter. I wish we had more time to prepare you but Winter is aware of your presence and we must act now! She only occupies the Northern terrain of Rastaland. We would have sent her away long a go but she was binded to you with her spell! Yet, I have confidence in our victory. Us coming down upon them like a bolt from the blue and the numerous service arms and beings shall hand us the conquest. You will be under Rasta Rabbits, Forrest Fairies and our drill guard's protection, though you will not perform in combat your presence here is our strength. Winter knows her defeat is next! You may observe the battle from above I will signal you when to descend!"

After concluding his talk with Layla, King Osiris and Queen Isis of fire took to the sky surrounded by guards and Regulators and a slew of other Rastaland beings headed to war!

Taking the form of an eagle with Rasta colored wings Rasta Rabbit glided in sync with his comrades heading to battle. When they arrived in Ivory Heights Rasta Rabbit located an empty spot in the sky to hover in and shot to it. Layla had shape shifted into a Rasta fly and perched herself upon his shoulders, her Rasta colored wings bellowing in the breeze. Drifting over the scene, Layla observed the Rasta Renegades closing in on The Ivory Towers.

Winter and her ice-cold gang were caught off guard by the attack, Winter knew Layla being in Rastaland meant war, but she thought she had additional time to strategize and obliterate other minds during their fasting. But the occasion had arrived, insanity in the details.

Winter monitored the exact confrontation as Layla from a safe view atop Ice Mountain. Policed by her two closes goons, Titan a monstrous polar man and Corrupt a half dragon half sea monster. Winter watched the Rasta Renegades infiltrate her queendom like an avalanche, faulting Layla having her love stone as one of the reasons her guard was down!

The Rasta Renegades surrounded the Ivory Towers from all ends; sky, ground and water, the fire from their spirits dissolving Winter's eons of ice. Her Regulators and Witches were no match for the unstoppable force that assaulted their beings, caught unaware they had no time to plan, cast spells, read minds or run!

Once the gates were down the Rasta Renegades entered Winter's palace and pulverized everything in sight! The order given by Osiris stated: 'Buit aan blik!' 'Martar el tiempo!' 'Kill on sight! A time to Kill!' In every dialect of Rastaland to beings and comrades alike.

With the assistance of their allies. The Rasta Renegades killed every creature in Ivory Heights but Winter and her two guards who thought they were safe at the top of Ice Mountain. Once all beings were exposed. The King and Queen of Rastaland entered Ivory Heights. Isis had waited centuries for this moment! To confront Winter! To find her father! This was the beginning of the end of Winter and Isis breathed in the significance of their juncture.

"WINTER!" shrieked Isis

All of Rastaland heard her name including Winter who materialized in front of Isis, guards in tow.

"Yes lil sistah?" answered a sarcastic Winter surveying the abandoned colony that once was Ivory Heights.

"It's over Winter! Encima!!! Where is my father!?" demanded Isis

"Where is your daughter?" asked Winter staring into the eyes of her mother Tapoah and her eldest sister Cleo who'd arrived shortly after the King and Queen, King Osiris was behind Isis but Winter expected to see Layla as well.

"Where is your conscience?" shouted Isis "I'm almost afraid to decipher your memories because of all that I'm going to find!" Isis continued her dark skin glowing, her eyes of fire.

"You'll never..." before Winter could complete her thought aloud, Isis performed an abracadabra move impressing all that witnessed.

"Memories of Truth!" Isis said, speaking slowly and very calmly. The essence of fire filling the atmosphere, she lifted her arms spinning around on one leg she turned chanting 'Memoria un verdad!' Winter's guards Titan and Corrupt stood on either side of Winter in a sleep induced trance, Winter's red eyes closed and she fell into Isis' conjuration of truth.

"Where is our father?" Isis asked as she continued spinning.

"Neptune's inner moon Triton." Winter answered easily enough under Isis spell.

Tapoah, Cleo and guards exited immediately to retrieve Boaz. Winter had held her father captive on Neptune's moon for seven hundred seasons in Rastaland time.

To Ice Mountain
Subservient to my fire fountain restraints
Sistah Saint
Turned wintery witch
Big sister turned bitch
Your reign in Rastaland is over
My daughter whose over my shoulder
Shall seal your fate
Extirpate your spells
Claiming her rightful place
As the Queen that dwells
In the dimension like no other
For she is our Rasta Soul Sistah, Rasta flower daughter,
Birthed by her queen Mother!
Who has discovered her place
Despite your mental restraints
You who infiltrated my gates
Getting comfortable here your epic mistake
Kidnapping my father, you're a family disgrace
Face to face

You must be set free
Leaving Rastaland eternally!"

Isis finished her pertinent poem while chanting 'Fuego circulo'
(*Circle of fire*).

Winter and her bandits Titan and Corrupt were swept up in a gust of wind fire that was Isis' spell. They were launched to the top of Ice Mountain the entire mountain was encircled by fire.

The Rasta Renegades continued to patrol Ivory Heights. Layla looked as if she was in a daze gazing at Isis's rotating rapture. She'd observed the encounter in angst! Fully comprehending all that Winter had stolen from her. She should have been there all along, preserving her utopia. There was still so much for her to unearth in Rastaland, yet she had been on earth instead of her motherland! She knew she'd missed centuries of tutelage and not to mention love due to her aunt's wickedness. And to think she could have been lost on earth forever had her family not been persistent in their pursuit! This fueled Layla's spirit for what she knew was next.

"You must return to the Golden Temple to pray and prepare with Ras Fela" said her father King Osiris flying beside her and Rasta Rabbit in their eagle forms. Rasta Rabbit nodded his comprehension and began to trail King Osiris towards the Golden Temple. Layla gripped his feathers in her Rasta fly form primed for war! Already in prayer!

CHAPTER THIRTEEN: GOLDEN GROUND WORK

When they reached the Golden Temple Layla shape shifted into a human wearing the golden gown she'd fasted in before the battle. King Osiris escorted Layla down the path leading to the Temple, the guardian angel greeted them as they approached, her cloudy eyes mystifying Layla.

"Ras Fela will receive you in the inner court" she stated nodding her golden head while flitting her wings a bit.

King Osiris kissed Layla's cheek and pushed her towards the entrance stepping behind her. Layla crossed the threshold of the Temple, perforating the golden aura she perambulated down the aisle towards Ras Fela who lit incense in a colossal holder that caressed the ceiling.

Welcoming one another with a hug, Ras Fela took hold of Layla's arm leading her around the right side of the Temple onto its grounds. Inside the Temple they had not spoken, the Golden sanctuary had that kind of influence on you. It was a place of worship and meditation, the Rastaland beings prayed, fasted and held different celebrations and feast there. Upon penetrating the Tabernacle you were promptly enveloped in the devotion and exaltation of the Lord. The Rastaland population came to praise and honor God, to thank God for the sun, the moons, earth and other planets, dimensions and galaxies. They took time out of everyday to gather and glorify God! Everyone in Rastaland had a golden seat in the Temple, and this adoration was always experienced and respected. God was first and revered in Rastaland.

Once outdoors, Ras Fela began to counsel Layla on what was happening and what was next. They sat beneath a baobab tree as Ras Fela began to speak;

"When the sun sets once I've explained everything you shall cleanse yourself before reentering the Temple and fasting into the next moon in preparation for your confrontation with Winter. Our mother Isis has placed her under a spell placing her upon Ice Mountain; yet you must defeat her to break the makutu on you and our grandfather, Mama can't hold her there forever! Once you've defeated her in battle she will have no choice but to retreat. Her magic will hold no power!" exclaimed Ras Fela.

"She will die as a being here going to God leaving Rastaland forever never to return eternally excommunicated. Winter has always been at odds with our mother, she has used you as a pawn for far too long. It ends now!" Ras Fela said, growing more and more excited.

"She knows that you will become Queen of Rastaland, inheriting the powers of our mother and father, you shall reign as ruler! As I have appointed our father and mother, you shall crown your children as ruler of Rastaland! This is all yours Layla! And once you leave the Temple, after your fast you will turn twenty-one the next moon, an adult in Rastaland as well as earth. Yet here as Princesa your powers shall multiply now and every year from now. One day you shall be the most supreme sorceress in all the planets. For there are Princesses who have been training since the beginning of time and will always be more masterful. Yet you shall rank amongst the best! And my time in Rastaland is coming to an end; tenacity shall transform my being, so now it is imperative that you are thoroughly groomed by our parents," said Ras Fela.

"Removing Winter is your first step in ruling Rastaland, once the wicked witch is eliminated you may sustain a concrete learning pattern, no longer deterrent by evil distractions. The reason our mother placed her big sister Winter atop Ice Mountain is her heart is there! Winter placed her heart at the top of Ice Mountain when she infiltrated the Northern Terrain of Rastaland. After the death of Seth, the love of her life, she became viler, abducting you and our grandfather! Sending you to earth where our aunt Cleo could protect you but never break Winter's spell over you! She has taken so much from you, time, education; she has caused our family so much suffering. Yet you must forgive her with your soul, abolish her physically. Allow my words to fuel your fire, may your fast inspire your expeditious victory!" concluded Ras Fela.

Ras Fela then ushered Layla to a bath house where they cleansed themselves. Bathing in golden water inside golden tubs in a purifying bath house for that purpose. The water smelled of rose petals leaving Layla's skin radiant. Ras Fela then guided Layla back inside the Temple, the sun began descending as they knelt before the altar in prayer. Layla closed her eyes and allowed God into her soul she was a lioness of God! God's warrior! And it was time to shine and as she'd been told, claim her rightful place!

Meanwhile, Osiris and Rasta Rabbit safeguarded the area wher Isis was located. A tornado inferno, the flames wrapped around the mountain. A wall of fire that Winter could not penetrate, still under Isis's conjuration, powerless.

Osiris and Rasta Rabbit began to converse about Layla's progress to pass the time.

"You believe Layla is prepared?" Osiris asked Rasta Rabbit.

"Yes, after seeing and being in her home again, reviewing her past lives, shape shifting and participating in a mock battle, I think she knows who she is!" replied Rasta Rabbit confident in his training and Layla's faith in herself.

"You're positive?" questioned Osiris.

"Yes! You should have saw her in the ring! She shape-shifted! Becoming an owl, soaring high and shooting fire from her wing!" reported Rasta Rabbit.

"I saw a bit, but you're the *wind beneath her wings* so to speak, she is very comfortable with you! You won't be on that mountain with her!" said Osiris.

"She believes Sire, when reviewing her past lives she glimpsed the true reflection of her past self." replied Rasta Rabbit.

"King, we have Reefa D here! Captured and brought in front of you as you ordered." interrupted the Captain of the Rasta Renegades, proud his team had delivered.

Standing seven feet in his Rasta colored uniform, a clean-shaven lion, his badges of honor sparkled in the sun. He held Reefa D in front of him by the arm, Reefa D's hands were locked behind his back in diamond cuffs.

"We cast our configuration desist spell so he will refrain from shape shifting Sire!" continued the Captain.

"Good, we wouldn't want you turning into a bird and flying away from our confrontation, now would we?" Osiris asked Reefa D.

Reefa D stared at Osiris in disgust, his eyes red from the charm placed upon him, he looked into the sky, yearning to be there, then back at Osiris, silent.

"I don't expect you to cry nor beg for your life, I can just throw you in the fire and be done with this!" suggested Osiris, looking in the sky, then at the fire behind him where Isis was and back at Reefa D.

"I should have never trusted the White Witch Winter." answered Reefa D humbly, a handsome male being; tall, human form, brown skin, big owl eyes, dirt and blood staining his shirt.

"Why would you ever sale white ice! It destroys you! Created by Winter, a substance of death! All her allies use it! I never understood, when we have the best ganja in the cosmos growing everywhere you look!" replied Osiris.

"Then I thought nothing of the consequences, I used white ice to control others as Winter did, I wouldn't blame you if you threw me in the fire! I betrayed you by siding with Winter." said Reefa D.

"You also attempted to filter that acid cessation into my army, being one of my top soldiers at the time of your demise." said Osiris, reminding Reefa D of other wrong doings he'd rather forget.

"Not to mention trying to block Layla when she and Rasta Rabbit were on there way to see Judasemi." continued Osiris, with his onslaught of Reefa D's errors in judgment.

"I didn't try to block her! That's why they didn't kill me along with the others! You think I was trying to stop them!" Reefa D yelled looking at Rasta Rabbit for sympathy and assistance.

"You caused Layla to stop! You could have ruined everything dipping into her mind like that!" retorted Rasta Rabbit.

"And yes, your sorry soul was saved for this moment!" Osiris said answering Reefa D's question.

"I needed to look you in the eyes before casting you to The Rasta Reformatory for seventy-seven seasons!" resumed Osiris.

"No!" yelled Reefa D "I could have told them Layla and the Rabbit was there but I didn't! I was in so much pain! I would never try to sabotage their plot! I wanted them to succeed." replied Reefa D, pleading for his life.

"You wanted them, us to succeeded? By turning against her father? Selling white ice throughout Rastaland for Winter, killing for Winter, controlling other beings for Winter! You have a funny way of rooting for the team your own!" said Osiris.

"I was on no one's team!" shouted Reefa D.

"And that was the problem! You weren't even on your own team! If you loved yourself maybe you wouldn't have abused others! Sorry rascal! You shall have plenty of time to think about your actions, loads of time to discover what your made of and whose team your on where your going!" said Osiris.

Reefa D and Osiris stared one another down for a few seconds.

"Raza!" shouted Osiris and Reefa D evaporated, his diamond cuffs clanging to the ground.

***

Reefa D materialized in the Field of Qualm's where vindictive vampires suck you dry if you didn't make it to the cabins before dust.

Walking through the Valley of Time, he could only shake his head at the consequences of his predicament.

At the end of the valley sat rows of cabins, filled with Rastalands convicted, serving time until their season was up.

Reefa D found the first three cabins he came to empty, he bumped into an inmate entering the fourth.

"Excuse me" said Reefa D to the young being he had bumped.

"No problem, I'm Dandela." greeted Dandela, he had burns on seventy five percent of his body, one eye on the side of his head, red spiky hair and no lips, his teeth protruding from his face.

Reefa D stood three inches taller than Dandela and tried not to stare directly into his face.

"Where is everyone?" asked Reefa D.

"In the lunchroom, its dinner time, Marlam is the head guard and he has been informed of your arrival!" replied Dandela proceeding to exit the cabin.

"Please, tell me what goes on here?" Reefa D asked.

"Who cast you here?" asked Dandela, walking back into the cabin to answer Reefa D.

"Osiris" replied Reefa D.

"Oh! Man! The king cast you here?" Dandela asked in disbelief.

"Yes, why are you so alarmed?" asked Reefa D.

"Because, Isis and Ras Fela usually send you here for a spell, excommunicate you from Rastaland, in that moment you decide where you want to go and that's it! But Osiris makes you stay here forever, most never make it to their free season, they choose to be killed!" explained Dandela.

"They rather die than stay here?" asked Reefa D.

"Yes! Osiris knows this, so instead of sentencing you to death he allows you to decide when you'll die. We are near the Present Forest, trapped in the present moment, stripped of our powers, no weed, just fixing machine parts day in and out." elaborated Dandela.

"Fixing parts and sleeping in cabins don't sound so bad." grinned Reefa D.

"Well, the vampires that bang on your window every night, preventing you from sleeping are bad, they can't get in, but they sound like they can! The sand and lightening storms are bad, the beings that make your life here a living hell are bad and the way the machine parts cut up your hands is the worst!" replied Dandela showing Reefa D his callous and cut fingers.

"I could go on but I think you're getting the picture. I was sentenced here by Ras Fela for setting my wife on fire, I tried to kill myself, its hard taking your own life! Why did Osiris cast you here?" asked Dandela.

"Because I sold white ice for Winter, I was one of his soldiers, and I also tried to get into the mind of Layla," answered Reefa D.

"His daughter!" shouted Dandela, cutting Reefa D off, his deep voice echoing out into the valley.

"Yes." replied Reefa D.

"She's back? She's back! I'm missing so much being stuck in here! And Ras Fela will exile me to Saturn my home, I won't get to meet her!" said Dandela sadly.

"I was trying to assist her! I wanted to meet her as well! But Osiris thinks I meant her harm! Like you said, I may never get out of here!" said Reefa D sliding down the wooden panel to the floor.

"Nope, they will keep a close eye on you here, especially since the King sent you! And he finally got his daughter back and thinks you tried to interfere! I'm surprised he didn't allow Isis to put her fire to you!" said Dandela, looking down at Reefa D where he sat.

"I'll find a way outta here or die trying!" said Reefa D coaching himself to stay positive.

"How long is your season here?" asked Dandela.

"Seventy-seven seasons is my sentence." replied Reefa D.

Dandela whistled.

"Most don't make it past their thirtieth or fortieth season, the majority allow the vampires to tear them apart, few have the courage to face their fears in exchange for their lives in The Valley of Time." said Dandela.

"Facing your fear?" repeated Reefa D.

"Yes, a hell worse than this one! Whatever you fear is magnified and you're stuck there until the spirits of time release you. You could be stuck in The Valley of Time longer than you're sentenced season! Really not a great option!" explained Dandela.

"I have to get out of here!" said Reefa D growing more anxious the more he discovered.

"Yes brother we must! We should check you in and eat before it gets dark! The night belongs to the vampires here at the Rasta Reformatory." said Dandela extending his hand to assist Reefa D to his feet.

Walking to the lunchroom the new-found friends continued their conversation.

"Why would you trust Winter? Everyone knows she's a snake!" asked Dandela.

"I was an idiot, she enslaved me once I was kicked out of the Rasta Renegades. I went to her for help and she locked me up!" answered Reefa D still shocked at Winter's audacity.

"You see, Osiris could have sent you here then." Dandela pointed out.

"Yeah, I was on the run, I suppose he could have captured me if he wanted to. Once he found out that Winter had barred me, he probably felt I got what I deserved. He sent me here for fucking with Layla." replied Reefa D.

"I agree" said Dandela.

"Did you get burned when you burned your wife?" Reefa D asked.

"Yes, a moon being who played with fire! I disfigured her

as well, an action I regret with all that I am. I fight every night not to go out and lay my life down to a vamp. I've served three seasons I have one to go and I have an early release to Saturn to care for my family, my mother is sick. It's over for me friend, scarred physically for life, my wife and children taken away, but you may be able to get through to Osiris during your hearing! Since his daughter is back, once everything settles, he may let you free!" Dandela said to encourage Reefa D as they entered the lunchroom.

"The Rasta Renegades killed Winter's entire army! They pulverized Pallid! I knew they left me alive for a hellish reason!" Reefa D stated taking in the Reformatories lunchroom.

Five hundred prisoners ate at glass benches and tables, some stood in line being served. Reefa D saw prisoners who ate like animals from their plates unable to use their injured hands.

Reefa D felt someone staring at him and looked to his left, it was a short being, every inch of his body covered in tribal ink, by the way he swung his machete, Reefa D knew this was the one and only Marlam, the prison guard.

Reefa D proceeded to the line with Dandela, he asked about Marlam, who was walking quickly over to where they stood.

"There's only one guard?" Reefa D asked Dandela, gesturing towards Marlam.

"Yes, only one is needed!" said Dandela.

Reefa D closed his eyes, trying to access his shape shifting abilities.

"Don't!" Dandela yelled into Reefa D's ear, warning him, knowing what he was up to.

"Halt!" yelled Marlam, throwing his hands into the air, a

yellow mist sprayed from his palms, floating to Reefa D, the vapor enveloped Reefa D and when the cloud lifted Reefa D was Dandela's twin!

Marlam's spell gave Reefa D more burns on his smooth face than Dandela had, and he could hardly see out of the one eye he now had on the right side of his face. He could not see his reflection but he felt hideous!

"Since you wanted to shape shift so bad, I didn't think you'd mine looking like your new best friend!" said Marlam standing four feet in his Rasta uniform, his aura sending a hush over the lunchroom.

Marlam walked up into Reefa D's face, staring him directly in his eye.

"Most are here because of foolish choices, you are no exception! And you will accede to every rule here or I will feed you to the vampires myself! Welcome to the Rasta Reformatory!" shouted Marlam, his spittle flying in Reefa D's face.

"Away!" Marlam commanded and Reefa D was dragged backwards by invincible forces to a cell adjacent to the dining room.

Caged in his new form and prison, all Reefa D's hopes ran out his eye, as he cried for the first mistake he ever made, trusting Winter! He prayed for a hearing soon with the rulers of Rastaland, living under these conditions was a fate unfathomable!

***

Osiris turned back to Rasta Rabbit after dismissing Reefa D.

"Now that he is where he belongs and Isis holds our final rival at the top of the mountain, I can only pray that Layla's moon day provides more power and strength, she must conquer Winter!" Osiris said to Rasta Rabbit.

"She will, she has faith!" said Rasta Rabbit.

"Yes faith!" smiled Osiris.

"That which you cannot see!" replied Rasta Rabbit.

"Yes, now I must have faith in her," said Osiris turning to face Isis. He looked to the sky and said a silent prayer of victory for his family.

CHAPTER FOURTEEN: LAYLA VS. WINTER

Layla fell into a deep spiritual state praying beside Ras Fela, giving thanks for her gifts and the acknowledgment of those gifts. Thanking God that she now knows her purpose. Exalting the King of Kings for being awake, aware, alert, alive, a...PRINCESA!

Pulsating through her spirit she could feel the sensation of her new-found cogency racing through her veins, brewing through her fingertips. Opening her eyes Layla realized she was alone in the asylum. Gathering herself after such a deep reflection, she traipsed up the golden path exiting the Temple.

Once outside the guardian Angel of the Temple called her name, addressing her and grabbing her attention.

"Layla" said the guardian Angel "I am keeper of the Golden Temple as you will be curator of Rastaland! Happy Rasta Earthday, I have a gift for you and a few instructions. First your gift since everyone loves gifts!" The guardian Angel blew her breath and a puff of smoke came out as a necklace dropped from thin air around Layla's neck. It was a gold chain with a black jade circle with red, gold, green and black swirling through the circle shaped charm. The symbol rotating in a circle around Layla's neck serving as it's axis. It was the same necklace that King Osiris wore.

"This necklace will protect you against every challenge you shall soon face, it has been handed down through generations and lifetimes. You will pass it on to your children one day. Circling your neck, your shield, any trauma will be sensed and your ancestors and army will be alerted. Now for your instructions," said the guardian Angel.

"First it's imperative your are well informed, because you will perform this mission alone, no Rasta Rabbit, no Ras Fela, no Osiris, no Isis of Fire. Isis will hold her spell on Winter until you've reached the bottom of Ice Mountain. Winter has to face you with the Rasta Renegades patrolling what once was Ivory Heights, there is no escape! NO assistance from family and friends!" as the guardian Angel spoke everyone appeared. Circling Layla, except Isis.

The guardian Angel continued, "You must utilize the gift and lessons you've learned. You must also place Winter's love stone. On her third eye, causing her to reconnect with her emotions. She projects her fear onto others instead of getting to the bottom of why she feels a certain way. Next you must reach into the top of Ice Mountain retrieve and dissolve her heart! While placing the love stone to Winter's third eye you must recite this poetic conjuration:

For the time you have robbed
Your now placed in the hands of God
As your spirit leaves may it refresh the memories of old
The memories you stole
I hold forgiveness
Bearing no malice
I except the challenge
To lead my people to the next trilogy
Their Queen eternally
From this moment forth you have been infinitely banned
Never again

Will you see Rastaland!

The guardian Angel burned the incantation into Layla's psyche. Rasta Rabbit, Ras Fela and King Osiris stepped aside to allow Layla to begin her journey.

The necklace that the guardian Angel gave Layla relieved her dubiety. Every time the charm circled her neck she felt empowered.

Layla was akin to the ambience of heated energy that throbbed beneath her skin. Rubbing her hands together, she used her clammy fingers to twist her dreadlocks into a ball on the back of her neck, getting them off her back. She was beginning to sweat. She believed and tapped into this potent raw sensation racing through her soul! Eager to shed her skin and soar in the cool breeze, Layla free-fell on faith, immersed in who she was in the moment!

"Layla" called the guardian Angel

"Yes" Layla answered turning back to face the guardian Angel.

"Be careful, don't be tricked by any of Winter's crafty games, don't eat or drink anything on Ice Mountain. Don't forget, once you've reached the base of the mountain your mother will end her spell and you will be on your own! Follow the Rasta fairies to Ivory Heights. Good luck Princesa, may Thee Creator guide and protect you!" wished the guardian Angel.

Layla thanked the guardian Angel as she kissed her father. Rasta Rabbit and Ras Fela wished her a happy birthday. She said a silent prayer and metamorphosed into a Rasta eagle following the Rasta fairies, she took flight towards Ivory Heights.

Layla shot out like a rocket into the sky, following the cool breeze and Rasta fairies she knew led to Ivory Heights. She hadn't been flying long when what remained of the Ivory Towers appeared. Isis spun around the tower in a dizzying circle. Layla took time before landing on the mountain to alert Isis of her presence.

"Mom, I'm here!" Layla said in her head looking at Isis who stopped spinning upon hearing Layla's thought. She pointed to where Layla should land on Ice Mountain.

Layla flew to the base of the mountain and altered her being from a Rasta eagle into a mountain cat. She became a beautiful black puma easily gripping the gravel and rock that made up the mountain. The alp was magnificent! Beautiful flowers and vines continued to grow despite the snow. Some of the flowers had what appeared to be weed and fruit growing from the tips. Ignoring the guardian Angels warning about eating anything, Layla bit some of the blue, banana-shaped fruit. It was sweet as its juices sprayed the inside of her mouth. It tasted like a grape. She was about to eat another piece when she saw the Rasta fairies shaking their heads warning her. Simultaneously she saw something move in her peripheral vision. Turning around, Layla came face to face with one of Winter's goons Titan!

"Hi" spoke Titan.

"You scared me!" exclaimed Layla transforming from the puma into herself, dressed in a Rasta jumpsuit and puma gym shoes.

"No need to be afraid, I was just trying to find a quiet spot to smoke," explained Titan lifting his hands to reveal a spliff in one hand and a lighter in the other.

"I thought Winter was the only one left in Ivory Heights, who are you?" questioned Layla.

"No one important, just trying to lay low until all this

blows over" said Titan lightening his joint.

"I like your shirt" Layla said to this Being, who resembled a polar bear on steroids, in a Bob Marley shirt!

"Oh! I love Bob!" smiled Titan with ugly monster teeth that would charm you he lifted his shirts one after the other. One T-shirt showed Bob Marley smoking a spliff with afro locks, the second was of Bob performing on stage, the third was of Bob playing soccer, the fifth was Bob's face with the words 'One Love' in red, gold and green letters running across, a sixth T-shirt was of Bob and the early members of the Wailer's, Peter Tosh and Bunny Wailer, and the seventh wasn't a shirt at all! A supernatural snake came out of Titan's belly towards a startled Layla who leaned back making both her hands machetes. They began to partake in a dance of death. Layla swiftly crossed her arms in front of her, decapitating Titan and his snake belly monster!

Using Bob Marley to trick her! He deserved to die on the spot! Layla converted back into her puma shape-shifting form and sprinted halfway up the mountain before Titan's body hit the ground.

Even in her puma formation she slipped down the icy mountain a few times, losing her claw grip. Getting a better grasp Layla pushed herself towards the top of the mountain.

She could see Corrupt, another one of Winter's nin-com-poop guards, pacing back and forth; Layla assumed he was patrolling this side of the mountain. Turning her paws into machetes again, Layla awaited her chance to attack, not wanting to be tricked a second time. Hiding behind a rock and some bushes Layla seized her chance when Corrupt came near. Wasting no time, Layla beheaded Corrupt, before his body hit the ground she had Winter's full attention. Running full speed Layla knocked the platinum witch down!

Winter was on the ground for only a second. She pushed Layla off her and rolled to her feet. She stood up and took her fighting stance. Legs apart, hands up, her mind ready to cast a spell!

"I see you've received your trinket, see if it can pro...," before Winter could finish Layla hit her in her left shoulder with a fire ball. Layla remained in her puma form finding it easier to move with her paws over the ice.

"You little witch! Off with your locks!" shouted an enraged Winter. She didn't think her niece had it in her!

Winter and Layla tousled, Winter used some of the fire power she had stored and stolen from Steward Suns to blast Layla in the face. Layla, being a Sun Presence, was unaffected by the flame, merely stepping away, the burns disappearing within seconds. Deploying her witchery, Winter transformed into a polar bear, like her thug Titan. She pounced on Layla. Aunt and Niece commenced to duke it out towards the mountains edge. Winter was on top of Layla, Layla looking for an opportunity to flip Winter over; when the thought of becoming a fly and flying away came to mind, she looked up to see a being made of water rushing up behind Winter.

A heavy tap on her shoulder, rendered Winter speechless, turning to stare into the dark green eyes of Seth Waters and the eyes of fire that belonged to Steward Suns, Winter stood baffled by their presence, as she rolled off Layla, getting quickly to her feet.

"Seth? Steward?" questioned a breathless Winter.

"Habari Gani, bitch mbaya, simama sasa Winter! (*Good morning, evil bitch, stop now Winter!*), I have come from the portal you named 'The Land of the Lost!'" explained Steward.

"Hoe? Wanneer? (*How? When?*)," asked a flustered Winter, her eyes telling a story of old.

"Lana, dada yako! (Lana, *your sister*)" explained Steward he stood tall and malevolent in his bearing. In his human form his brown skin glistened, his shoulder length locks flowing in the wind. Winter recoiled from the sheer essence of his nine foot being.

"Je moet het. Loslaten kaskazini van Rastaland! Je moet de heks stoppen, Layla ni Princesa wetu na Malkia! Je bent een duivel! Na tunakaribia kuwakaribisha kwako! (*You must let go of the North of Rastaland, you must stop witch, Layla is our Princesa and Queen! You are a devil! And we close our welcome to you*)," continued Steward in a mixture of Swahili and Dutch, a vernacular Winter and her goons created.

Layla stood in her puma stance ready to pounce, not perceiving the dialogue but grasping the stealth resilience between the two. Giving her a moment to catch her breath and beating heart!

"Een Seth-baby, het spijt me mijn liefde! (*An Seth baby, I'm sorry my love!*)," exclaimed Winter turning to face Seth.

Seth Waters wavered over Winter, Steward and Layla, in his liquid configuration he stood twelve feet; his body resembling a mortal with skin of water, his hands were claw vessels, his eyes hate, his voice raw!

"Nibusu," said Seth. Addressing Winter, saying 'kiss me' in Swahili. Winter began to levitate until she was face to face with the love of her life.

Once she reached eye level, Seth greeted her once more.

"Kusubiri dada, inanyesha katika nyumba yako, kuwakaribisha hadi mwisho!! Geen shukrani, Geen leven! Je bent niemand loyal. (*Wait sister, it's raining in your home, welcome to the end! No appreciation, no life! You are loyal to no one.*)," spoke Seth.

"Wat bedoel je geen leven? Werkelijk? (*What do you mean*

no life? Really?)," interrupted Winter.

"Wat bedoel je geen leven? Werkelijk? (*What do you mean no life? Really?*)," mimicked Seth "Niemand zal meer door jou lijden, boze koningin, ik lijd aan de pijn in mijn hart vanwege jou! (*No one shall suffer because of you anymore, evil Queen, I suffer from the pain in my heart because of you*)."

For the first-time Layla witnessed Winter being afflicted by someone else. She could sense the love Winter had for this being. They made beautiful magic as their souls flittered between the two, Seth a monster body of water and Winter a levitating fairy of frustration.

"Kill her!" Layla shouted intervening and breaking into their conversation, Seth turned his attention to the talking puma that was Layla and addressed her firmly.

"Princesa" Seth began,

"You must recognize what your mind refuses to visualize

look into my eyes

realize

all that your aunt has compromised!"

Rhymed Seth, clapping his liquid limbs a flash of light blinded Layla.

She was inside of Seth's mind, reliving his memories, Layla was immersed in their first encounter, meeting Winter in chemispell class, Layla could feel that Seth was intrigued by this mysterious woman. Layla saw that Winter was no longer lonely when Seth arrived, she threw all of her love into him. And through Seth's vision, Layla witnessed everything from love making to their first fight. Winter and Seth's love was a roller coaster ride of emotions for them both. Winter was no longer alone, no longer vulnerable, Seth showed her it was okay to love, so his betrayal derailed all that they had built together.

Layla observed their intense final moment, Seth's compassion for this other being, ignorant of his unfaithfulness, young and full of lust, Layla could sense his hunger for life, his thirst for his future. And the scream! Winter's scream, when she caught Seth cheating that fatal day was brutal! It sounded like twenty-seven guns, a billion fire works, a tornado alert and every siren on earth going off in unison. When Seth shattered so did their love, Layla also realized Winter had been pregnant at the time of Seth's demise!

After Seth's death, Layla could still see Winter as Seth could, though he was now in another form he could still monitor Winter's behavior. Layla watched Winter kidnap her grandfather Boaz and kill her daughter! Layla studied Winter performing her own abortion! Pulling the still born child from her body, outside on the deck of her home, bashing the dead child to blood and mush with a block of ice.

"You murdered your own child!? Why?" Layla said, coming out of the trance Seth had her under.

"Because she's shetani! Evil, you should have asked why she is so evil!" answered Steward Suns for Winter. He watched the whole memory as well. Familiar with Winter's history, Steward was aware of her treacherous ways being a victim himself.

"Call me what you like while being cloaked in ice!" Winter shrieked using her powers she shot water from her wrist encasing a stunned Steward, she then threw his being into the sky over the mountain. Winter still levitating, kept her good eye on Seth, awaiting his reaction!

"You were always quick with your hands and evil with your heart" joked Seth. "How could you kill our daughter?" he asked more seriously.

"You killed her when you betrayed me! I could never birth our love child when there was no love left!" yelled Winter.

"Well, our daughter did not survive this realm, but she has been successful in others" informed Seth.

"Our daughter?" gasped Winter, never one to dwell on her hurtful pass actions, Winter never considered the fact of Seth seeking their daughter.

"Ja, onze dochter leeft nog! (*Yes, our daughter is alive*)," Seth shouted becoming a body of recollection his form transmitting his powers of retention. Winter and Layla watched Selah, Winter and Seth's daughter become a moon being on Neptune. She was artful and naturally beautiful in her form, lightening the way for other's she loved her clan and look forward to becoming a prodigious member of their dynasty.

"In order for her to live in physical form, becoming a water element and moon being, aware of herself outside of the light, one of her parents must sacrifice themselves, we must also be united to complete the task" spoke Seth ending his memory and bursting his throat open with his hands that were clawed machetes! As his being gushed rushing forth, Selah, the daughter of Seth and Winter stepped forth.

Her skin glistened, kissed by the sun, sparkling like diamonds, her eyes water, her locks hitting her waist, skin of libations, she floated to Winter and kissed her on the mouth.

"Nibusu" (*Kiss me*) said Selah to Winter, after they kissed, Selah begin clapping her hands, a Rasta colored unicorn appeared by her side, mounting her heavenly horse she addressed Winter once more. "Zie je volgende leven moeder! (*See you next life mother!*)." Her voice sounded like running water over rocks.

"Wat" (*What*) whispered Winter, stunned by the sight of her child.

Layla, observing the bewildered look on Winter's face, internalizing all that manifested before her eyes. She chose this moment to get even more physical with her nemisis, seeing Winter's shoulders hunched in defeat, viewing her daughter took the fight out of her.

Remaining in her puma formation, Layla threw a ball of fire from her right paw, aiming at Winter's head, catching the front of her hair on fire.

Winter waved her hands of water, threw her mane, extinguishing the flames. Using the pain from seeing her family for a few moments and then being ripped away again. Winter charged at Layla full speed! Dropping her jar of fire in her haste!

Winter slung Layla over the edge, shape-shifting saved Layla's life as she became a Rasta eagle, seeing her father Osiris flying over head, reminding her of her shape shifting ability. Layla became a Rasta Eagle flying back onto the mountain striking Winter in the face.

Being attacked by Layla in her eagle form, Winter lost her footing, slamming into the mountain busting open the back of her head, losing her polar bear formation she became a bleeding Winter. Layla converted into an Alligator Regulator pulling Winter by her locks to the top of the mountain where Winter's heart was.

Once Layla reached the top she pulled Winter's love stone from her pocket placing it to Winter's forehead. Winter was trying to resist Layla's choke hold, but Layla held firm, fueled with the anger she had towards Winter for taking her childhood, her life! Layla's eyes were fire so Winter couldn't cast a spell; she knew the beginning of the end was near.

Weakened by losing her daughter again, reconnected to the pain of losing Seth and that love stone scream! Piercing her ears and soul, Winter gave in, the war was over! She smiled up at Layla.

Warming the love stone with her internal inferno Layla placed the stone on Winter's third eye with one hand and begins chanting the spell poem from the guardian Angel;

"For the time you have robbed
Your now placed in the hands of God
As your spirit leaves may it refresh the memories of old
The memories you stole
I hold forgiveness
Bearing no malice
I except the challenge
To lead my people to the next trilogy
Their Queen eternally
From this moment forth you have been infinitely banned
Never again will you see Rastaland"

With her other hand, Layla reached into the top of Ice Mountain snatching out Winter's heart, melting it with her hands of fire!

Winter screamed as she dissolved beneath Layla's grasp, as Winter melted so did the icy atmosphere of Ivory Heights!

Layla watched in awe as the snow stopped and melted away leaving green growing grass. The air warmed up and all the ice of Ice Mountain rushed down the rocks into the river below. The sun danced above her and no clouds could be seen, flowers opened and blossomed before her eyes and birds and beings could be heard flying above.

Layla slipped on the defrosting ice beneath her causing her to fall backwards. It felt as if she was being pulled by some hypothetical force, she could grab hold of *NOTHING*, water and ice slipping through her fingers. She could no longer shape- shift!

Osiris, Isis and Rasta Rabbit clapped from the Rasta Skies, elated to see Layla dying in her Earth form. They knew she would return to them forever! There search for her on Earth had ended

***

Layla flew off the mountain on her back! Desperately trying to transform into a bird, a cloud, anything! With no such luck!

Too terror stricken to scream or change positions, God forbid landing head first! Yet back first didn't really appeal to Layla either.

Layla could now remember everything! Chasing the Rasta Bees through her labyrinth, running out the back of the maze into Winter's waiting arms. Winter flying her to her palace in Ivory Heights, wrapping her in moss leafs that smelled of mud. Sending her through a portal to earth, where she had been bound to human law, powerless, losing more of her memory each lifetime she returned to the planet of love and chaos, just to fear dying again.

She remembered her families love, Ras Fela's steadfast love in Holland, her father's compassion in Africa and Isis! Reminding her who she was in this life and Cuba!

Layla could see Isis! She stretched out her hand and yelled 'Mama!' at the top of her lungs. But she was falling further away from Isis' open arms!

The wind slapped her face and tears from her eyes, Layla

closed them tightly mentally maneuvering her spirit praying for the best!

Hearing grass rustle beneath her Layla opened her eyes she was back in Mt. Airy woods, sitting on a tree trunk, cold blunt in hand!

"OMG!" Layla thought standing up and looking around, she was exactly where she was before she was sucked into the weed stalk for what seemed like eons ago!

Where was the weed stalk? Where was Rasta Rabbit? Where was Rastaland? Was it all a dream? Was the weed she'd been smoking mind-blowing grade, instead of high-growing grade?

And to think she was just a Princesa who'd fulfilled her mission, killing her nemesis, liberating Rastaland! What an alluring illusion! How she wished it had been real! Damn!

Layla threw her joint on the ground angrily stomping off, exiting the woods. The entire walk she prayed the ginormous weed stalk would suck her back in! Taking her back to a place that felt like home! The magic, shape-shifting, flying! What an enchanting reverie! What an influential abode Rastaland had been. Layla couldn't wait to get home and write everything in her journal. She missed Rastaland already! Hoping she wasn't late for the exhibit because of her day dream, she high tailed it down the path.

Layla exited the woods and located her vehicle she was at her driver's door when she was shoved from behind. Layla turned around coming face to face with a hazel eyed woman who favored the White Witch Winter of Rastaland! She had platinum locks like Winter but she wasn't as majestic as she was in Rastaland. Despite her eyes being hazel not red as before her clothes were torn and raggedy and she smelled of body odor and garbage.

"Yo keys!" the woman demanded.

"What!?" exclaimed an alarmed Layla.

"Yo keys witch!" yelled the deranged woman.

"No!" Layla howled in response.

And quicker than you can say 'Rasta Rabbit' the woman pulled out a twenty-two caliber gun from beneath her baggy jacket, wasting no time she cocked the weapon and shot Layla at close range in her chest. Layla never saw the gun but the force of the bullet ripped through her heart, knocking her off her feet!

Layla was falling again! Her stomach dropping and doing somersaults, she kept her eyes shut at first, but when she felt the air pressure around her shifting she opened them.

The light was so bright she closed them again, from what she saw it seemed she was falling through light! Layla's skin began burning! She opened her eyes and the bright light had become fire! Was this hell? Layla's heart dropped and she begin to pray to the God of her understanding, humbly repenting.

Layla heard applause! She opened her eyes again for the third time, petrified of what she might see next!

She was in the Golden Temple in Rastaland! She was dressed in a golden translucent dress, Rasta colored gloves, shoes and crown! Her crown was incrusted with red, gold, green and black diamonds! She felt the fire pulsating through her veins and was liberated by it! And around her neck was her charm from the guardian Angel rotating.

The Golden Temple was filled with the citizens of Rastaland! Every being that resided in Rastaland made it to the Temple to praise God for bringing their Princesa home!

The crowd continued to celebrate and cheer as Layla gathered her bearings, she'd gotten her wish! She was home!

Back in Rastaland! Layla praised the Almighty for his many blessings!

"Layla" spoke the King of Rastaland Osiris, silencing the audience "Please come forth" He continued.

Layla strolled down the golden path that lead to the Temple's alter, standing at the altar in a circle facing Layla was King Osiris, Queen Isis of fire and a manly looking Rasta Rabbit! Layla smiled stopping in front of her parents.

"Layla" began Queen Isis of fire, "You went back to earth so that Winter, who shot and killed you there, could break her spell over you! She had to kill you on earth and direct your soul to Rastaland since she's exiled you there! The Almighty God assisted us in guiding your soul back to Rastaland, may his will be done always! God has blessed us! We can only want, desire, wish, God can makes it our reality! And now we'll be together forever! Winter is gone for good! And Rastaland is free of her sorrows! God is good!"

All of Rastaland including Layla clapped and thanked God for his mercy and blessings!

"Yes, Layla" King Osiris added, "Thee Creator has always aided us in watching over you! In this life on earth he blessed you with Robert or Rasta Rabbit!"

Layla smiled so hard her cheeks ached!

"Si Princesa! It was me all the time! On earth those few years with you as your boyfriend Robert and your guide here in Rastaland as myself Hoot A Gin Rasta Rabbit! I told you we would get to the bottom of that yearning in your belly together! And I knew you would go to the forest if I insisted you didn't! You are so predictable in that way! So, planting the stalk was easy! And you must know that when you destroyed Winter, you broke the spell on you and your grandfather!" explained a handsome smiling Rasta Rabbit. Who was tall and built like

Robert, brown like coffee, beautiful teeth and hands, she was going to love getting to know Robert/Rasta Rabbit all over again!

Layla felt a tap on her shoulder and turned to hug her grandfather Boaz, she felt so much love in his strong arms she felt safe! Boaz wrapped his hands around Layla's face and begins to speak for the first time to his granddaughter!

"Layla, Winter has taken nothing we can't replace! Before we begin our fast and home celebration, Ras Fela would like to speak with you outside." Boaz concluded placing his hands over Layla's eyes.

Layla's eyes were covered in darkness by her grandfather Boaz's hands, when the shadow of his hand lifted Layla was outside of the Temple in the warm Rastaland sunlight.

"Ras Fela! Brother!" Layla called loving how her ensemble sparkled in the sunlight, she was just about to ask the guardian Angel of the Temple where Ras Fela was when a Rasta fly landed on her shoulder.

"Ras Fela?" Layla asked the Rasta fly.

"Yes" Ras Fela answered flicking his wings.

"You're a Rasta fly now?" questioned Layla.

"Well, when we met in my garden I was a… what did you call me?...a man a pillar? Well now I'm a Rasta pillar turned Rasta fly! And I'll spread my wings until I die! It's time for me to head off for awhile! Now that the evil has been revoked, our Princesa, my little sister, has returned along with our grandfather. I, the founder of Rastaland, your dear brother, must set off and see what more there is to see! I shall visit again! In the meantime take care of our kingdom make babies with Rasta Rabbit learn how to become a leader claiming your rightful place! And above all put Thee Creator first and nothing will ever block your blessings or prosperity! I love you

Princesa, stay blessed and wise!" Ras Fela.

"When will you return?" Layla asked Ras Fela, rubbing her fingers along his beautiful colored wings. She had just returned, it was too soon for him to leave, she missed him already!

"I will come to check on everyone from time to time. Now I want to thank our allies who assisted in our victory, party on Jupiter and discover more of this vast universe. Once you get the hang of things, you can come and visit me anywhere I am anytime you like!" assured Ras Fela.

"I love you brother, see you soon!" said Layla.

"I love you too little sister!" replied Ras Fela.

And with that Ras Fela took to the Rasta skies! Layla watched until he blended in with the celestial sphere hugging herself she thanked God and vanished back into the Temple!

Layla learned a lot from her parents and loved ones, she made babies with her husband the Rasta Rabbit and Layla always put Thee Creator first, becoming one of the greatest queens in the universe!

And if you look with your soul's eye you can see traces of Rastaland everywhere you smoke!

THE END

THE EPILOGUE

It was August 21, 2017 on planet Earth, the day of the return of the total eclispe. A total eclipse hasn't been seen on Earth since Febuary 1979 and another won't appear until June 2024!

So, for many this was the last total solar eclipse of their lifetime, a very stellar diminution. Layla would have been 27 years old in her current human life form.

In Rastaland it was the season of Peret and the Rasta sun danced in the winter sky. Peret was Rastaland's winter season but since the exile of ther Winter Witch, the winters were more like Akhet, their rainy season, a bit of snow here and there. The ice, hail and heavy snow escaped along with Winter's exit.

Layla was 24 in Rastaland time, pregnant with her first child; her life was now, New Year's Day every morning. Nights filled with love, gatherings and laughter. Layla married 'Robert' Rasta Rabbit, she loved calling him that, loved knowing he would be at her side for as long as they wanted to be a part of one another's lives.

Layla wanted her union with Robert to mimic the love of her parents, Osiris and Isis. Their love extended beyond time, deep in the heart of what they shared, time didn't exist. Yes, they may have separated from time to time, as Layla learned during late night sessions with her mother. But, they always found a way back to each other in every life and chose to remain together for infinity………………….

***

A lot had changed. Layla, smiled to herself as she rode her Rasta hot wheel bike, a two-wheeled machine, painted red, black, gold and green. Riding through Tree Park to reach her Labyrinth before taking to the skies with her Mom and Aunt Cleo to watch the Moon Beings magic motions. The Beings nodded at Layla as she made her way through the vast park. Her baby bump visible as her yellow sundress bellowed in the Rasta breeze, "Thank Thee Creator for shorts", Layla thought.

Her mind returned back to her husband, who guided her back here and made an oath to protect her with his life before he even was sent to Earth to retrieve her. Robert Rasta Rabbit was now a member of the Rasta Renegades, making his way up the ranks. Her brother Ras Fela and father Osiris saw the warrior in him that they needed to accomplish their 'Lost Layla' mission.

Through his loyalty to her, his consistent and unwavering love she knew why he had been chosen. She knew that their love would last forever like that of her parents. Layla also knew that her parents felt he would be a good husband to her once his mission was completed; she was glad that everyone that loved her followed their hearts and brought her back home!

Layla could see why Winter would want to run Rastaland! Rastaland was Layla's home, her haven. Literally, her heaven! Layla had many experiences in the last three and a half moon cycles she'd been back in Rastaland. One of the most joyous moments was visiting Thee Creator in the realm of the absolute. The thought of being in Thee Creators presence still brings tears to her eyes, chills down her spine and exaltation throughout her soul!

She now understands her soul's mission, who she is where she is, where she is going and who'll she be when she gets there!

But she is already where she'll forever want to be.

***

Once Winter was ostracized and the celebrations for her eternal banishment subsided. Layla settled into life in Rastaland.

Layla's Labyrinth was as big as two American cities she constructed her mansion and territory within her own puzzle. Her home was made of all glass; she always wanted to see her land when she first opened her eyes. It was also her job to fill her city with the things she wanted; her family had left the labyrinth barren anticipating her return.

Layla replenished her burough with her own library, cafés and shopping district, creating places for families to grow and children to play. Her family teased her that her labyrinth was tailored to human needs. Layla knew she could change anything at any time. However, everyone loved that she dedicated a space for only animals and vegetation. No beings were allowed in that part of the labyrinth. Some were from Rastaland but Layla brought a lot of animals and creatures from Earth to reside in her haven; elephants, whales, lions, birds, monkeys and the Cuban Macaw parrot from her past life there.

Layla spent her days training physically and mentally with instructors at the Community Center. Exploring her mind's magic and spells of sorcery, shape shifting, fire and mind control, and time travel in the City Tribe of Isis. All beings of Rastaland assisted their princess in many ways, ensuring she would succeed in everything she put her mind to.

Gaining confidence and changing her perspective made each experience a lesson and blessing.

After praying and training, Layla would bike, fly or transport herself mentally to the City of Osiris. As princess and inheritor of Rastaland, Layla learned the innerworkings that allowed Rastaland to function properly. Layla oversaw reviewing new members who wanted to reside in Rastaland. Auditing education policies, assuring repairs were being completed, and addressing and resolving pollution and environmental issues. Layla also spoke with invading Aliens and Beings who plopped down in Rastaland's realm for whatever reason. And lastly, keeping her eyes on objects that flew too close to her dimension.

Layla was assigned her own military crew she named the Black Panthers, in honor of Huey P. Newton, her gang consisted of humanoid panthers as did Ras Fela's, yet other Beings of many backgrounds were apart of Layla's troops as well. Huey Newton held a special place in Layla and Ras Fela's heart. Mr. Newton's face was imprinted on Ras Fela's Black Rushmore mountain. Tomorrow on earth August 22, 2017 the day after this monumentous total solar eclipse will be the 28th anniversary of Mr. Newton's death. Layla planned to celebrate with the Human Souls of past light, a party for the Earthly departed, and a dimension outside of Earth.

Layla only left the realm with Robert Rasta Rabbit or a member of her tribe. As she was not yet comfortable leaving alone. She feels one day she may become comfortable, yet the citizens of Rastaland can feel her nervousness each time she exists.

Nevertheless, leaving was so much fun! Oh! The adventures she and Robert Rasta Rabbit have always steal her breath away!

Layla and Robert Rasta Rabbit would drop in on Earth often, visiting different places, and assisting humans anyway they can; fucking with police, casting 'good cop' spells that cause officers to feel any pain they inflict upon any citizen for seven weeks. The spell only lasted seven weeks but the mental experience was imprinted in their brains.

***

One time Layla and Robert Rasta Rabbit were pulled over for driving while black and beautiful, she will never forget. Layla and Robert Rasta Rabbit always have the best of everything in all realms and dimensions. Why not? With their minds they can create anything they desire. On this occasion, Layla and Robert Rasta Rabbit had went back to visit friends and family they knew when Layla was Earth bound. Layla got to see her best friend Tracy Millen from her life then among other friends and family.

Driving a Koenigsegg Agera R down the highway after their visits, doing about one hundred fifty miles per hour, they were pulled over by a State Highway Patrol Trooper. Robert Rasta Rabbit advised that they mind travel back to Rastaland. Layla knew Robert Rasta Rabbit had police chases all the time on Earth, vanishing into thin air or a fenced wall to escape the pursuit.

Layla thought it was funny, but being Earth bound for so long she had a connection to the human-troubled beings of Earth. Being an Aboriginal African, seeing the treatment of her people turning into a civil war all over again, she wanted to give the police a piece of her mind! She explained this to Robert Rasta Rabbit as they waited for the cop to exit his cruiser, they didn't wait long. The officer jumped out of his vehicle and ran to the passenger door, yelling

"Roll down the window and turn off the car!", ordered the officer.

Layla looked in the rear window to see back-up officers arriving to the scene. Two other police cars were pulling up when Robert Rasta Rabbit rolled down the window, exposing a black face behind the wheel of such an expensive care, the white officer's breath was caught in his chest.

Layla could see the evil surrounding this man and his fellow Klan members as they approached. Layla told Robert Rasta Rabbit she would take the lead in his mind, he looked at her, when their eyes met the officer pulled out his gun and yelled,

"Turn off the car and step out of the vehicle!", yelled the officer.

Layla snapped her fingers, their car disappeared, and they now stood in front of the shocked officers. Layla pulled their guns from their grips, using her hand as a magnet; she slowed time down with her left free hand.

The officers stood there in shock! All three cops backed into each other trying to create a huddle of protection.

"Who or what are you?" asked the officer that pulled them over.

"Who or what the fuck are you to pull us over and pull out guns!? These guns that melt with just a thought from my mind. You would have killed us with them, just for driving while being black!", shouted Layla, now enraged.

"Well you were going over one hundred miles an hour Ma'am, that's ille…"

Layla interrupted the pudgy middle officer that spoke.

"To get your attention! That's why we were driving so fast! But shit we could have been just fucking walking; leaving a party, selling CD's and we would have gotten the same fucking treatment! And who am I? I'm tired of this treatment! Tired of protesting, dying, seeing our men in jail for life for weed that's basically legal here!", Layla speaking with even more authority.

"This system was created to enslave my people, but now you want to lower the jail time for heroin and meth because white people are the main people addicted to it now! Who cared when my people were addicted to crack! Our black men behind bars and our families are dying! Africans are enslaved all over the world! Social media put police brutality front and center, but the police still don't give a fuck! How can you serve and protect when you so scared and shooting motherfuckas all the time! Tired of paying taxes for you to beat my ass! Paying you to beat my ass?! And even if we did leave and America was all white, you'd still find a way to fuck with us, screaming White Power the entire time!", Layla continued.

"More back-up is coming" yelled an officer.

"No one is coming! And you won't repeat that this happened! You'll pretend that it didn't, you won't talk about it amongst yourselves. But deep down like every other bigot who distorted love into hate! Who truly hates themselves! Wait! You know, I would be scared too! Because when these black folks wake up and realize you've stolen their God, their minds, their very souls! The uprising will be REAL!!! See ya then officers!!", Layla yelled triumphantly.

With that Robert Rasta Rabbit jumped into the sky becoming a bird before the police officers' eyes. Layla stared into their eyes, casting her 'good cop' spell, she spontaneously combusted, becoming a ball of evaporating fire.

Layla knew what it was to be so deceived that you no longer knew who you were. The White Supremacists that run Earth have stolen the minds of her people, as Winter had stolen her memory, both were mind controlled.

Layla spoke with Thee Creator about this concern of hers

for her people of Earth and many more things when she visited God in the realm of the absolute.

To reach Thee Creator in the realm of the absolute Layla had to bathe and fast in The Golden Temple, then the Guardian Angel of The Golden Temple escorted her to thee deific dominion.

The Guardian Angel whose name was Guardian Angel Aaliyah of The Golden Temple, Layla learned, blew Godjah over her transporting her soul to her creator.

***

Layla was in bed, in the boat bed of Meenwa to be exact; she was in South Africa a place she had visited during her Earth bound life. She had enjoyed her time here in Africa with Meenwa, she sat up and called his name.

"He is not here" came a voice.

The voice seemed to be in her head and the room at the same time. Looking towards the window, Layla felt a ball of light come through, immediately falling to her knees and exalted! Tears of praise fell from her eyes as she realized she was in the presence of God! She cried so hard! And it was because this being that created her loved her so much! She felt that no matter what she had been, done, thought, experienced, Thee Creator loved her regardless.

"Stop crying my child", commanded God.

"I can't help it", cried Layla, trying to pull herself together.

"Well it will be hard to converse through your tears", said God.

"Ok, let me get a grip", said Layla collecting herself. Then she asked, "God, can you recede a little, your energy is so strong! Can you help me gather myself?". Layla cried more.

God's voice was calm and sure. Not female or male, just

resilient and articulate.

Layla began to feel calmer as soon as she made the request.

"What form would you like me to take before we begin?", God asked sweetly.

"My choice?" asked Layla, knowing God was everything she was and more, including a shape shifter.

"Yes, your choice", said God lovingly.

"A black panther with locks!" said Layla accustomed to speaking with talking Black Panthers of her own. Before her eyes the air in front of her converted into a regal black panther, with swaying black and blue dreadlocks, his eyes were purple.

"Ok" was all Layla could muster.

"Let's consider this a Godly therapy session, you can ask me anything you like", God informed her.

"Well first, I love you! I worship and thank you for my life, for the many lives I've lived and for the life I live now!" Layla bowed and exalted her Creator.

"You are always welcome my love, I live through you and enjoy our experiences as well", said God smiling at his creation.

"So, the realm of the absolute is in South Africa?" questioned Layla looking deeply into the purple eyes of the panther from her kneeling position.

"Ha, No, South Africa resides on Earth in the realm of the relative. I created this space for us here because I knew that you found your happy place there when you visited Meenwa during your Earth life. I wanted you to be comfortable, come down to your level, so to speak, during this exchange. You could barely contain my presence in this form, if I revealed to much of my realm the realm of the absolute, your mind in this state, wouldn't be able to handle it", said God.

"This is mind blowing", Layla acknowledged.

"What questions does your soul seek my child", chided God.

"Thank you for allowing me to return home, Can I remain in Rastaland eternally?", asked Layla.

"Well of course, You already know the answer to the questions you ask, as I know the answers and the questions before you ask them!", said God.

"Yes, but that's why I love Rastaland, I can visit God! Just to communicate like this or speak about another soul mission, if I desire to ever leave Rastaland, I won't!" exclaimed Layla.

"True, and yes as you've said you will remain in Rastaland for as long as your heart desires. And you can always come to me no matter your physical form or realm.", said God.

"Thank you again Jah! What will become of Earth?", Layla questioned.

"Earth! My dear sweet planet, the globe that ails your heart so, your heart tells me that's why we're here. Now that you know your outcome, you want to know theirs?", God asked.

"They seem to be regressing; the planet is so fragile so primitive and shallow. They seem to be self-destructing, my African kin still in bondage, the water, air, food polluted! Whales with plastic in their bellies, throwing garbage into space! Actually throwing garbage at God because they won't recycle self-created diseases. You have beings who have stolen you from your people!" Layla began to cry again, envisioning all that she encountered and endured as an Earth Being.

Layla was able to revisit past memories in the Past Forrest in Rastaland, she never wanted to return to Earth as a human, she'd rather float around other dimensions as a Higher Evolved Being.

"Sadly, Earth is very primitive, my teenage planet, but beings there are waking up! Free choice is what I've given everyone and I'll never thwart your will or punish you for making a choice I created for you. The planet is in the shape it's in because as a collective consciousness the people have decided that's how they want it! Same as the beings of your realm dwell in peace, yet the beings of your realm remember every lifetime, visit other dimensions and God in the realm of the absolute!", God paused allowing the words to sink in.

"Your African kin", God continued, "My melonated mini-me's will continue to thrive and die. They could never lose me, all paths lead back to me. Once they realize that the God of their understanding is allowing them to die for a reason they will seek me, putting away all that they have been taught, turning inwardly, a spiritual revolution will be unleashed."-God

"Throwing garbage at God?"-God

"Ok, I don't know if that's factual but I wouldn't put it pass those humans!", said Layla.

"Once Earthlings realize we are all one, their consciousness shall elevate and they will free themselves by changing their perspectives", said God.

Layla visits the realm of the absolute often. She also visits Ras Fela who when she last visited was on Neptune. They've partied in spheres she can't pronounce, accessing domains in crevices she never knew existed in the universe.

***

Layla delights in arriving at the Past Forrest, smoking a Past spliff and revisiting her arrival to Rastaland.

Layla was proud she retained so much so quickly, knowing that her families belief in her is now the belief she has in herself.

***

Everything is still so new to Layla she rarely sleeps; Robert Rasta Rabbit says she passes out mid-sentence instead.

Layla entered her labyrinth and biked to her home, waving at Hierba, grass gnome and defender of her labyrinth.

She doesn't think of Winter at all, not even now during winter season. After reviewing everything she has left Winter in the past memories, and the never forget jar in the Past Forrest.

Robert Rasta Rabbit is waiting for Layla as she pulls onto the path leading to their home. He kisses her and rubs her stomach.

"Welkom home babies!", smiles Robert Rasta Rabbit.

***

The moon dance was about to begin, Layla looked forward to the eclipse. She would take her place in the sun as a sun being, touching the moon as it passes.

She looked into Robert Rasta Rabbits eyes, one day they would rule this realm together. She looked forward to the birth of their son and heir to her throne. She wanted more children, to be the best empress she could be, to love her husband and family, making up for lost time. Checking in on her beloved earthlings from time to time and learning more about Rastaland every day.

Layla praised God, seeing a star twinkle brightly in the sky at that same moment. She would continue to put Thee Creator first, being in Rastaland was a perpetual reminder that Thee Creator, through her parents and beings of Rastaland were the reason she was in her rightful place.

***

As the moon eclipsed the sun, Layla's Aunt Cleo protector of Earth, absorbed the essence of the sunlight. Asking Thee

Creator for its continued protection, knowing that the human beings of Earth would persevere. Levitating in space she looked out onto the universe. She searched for Winter but only saw darkness, meaning Winter was with Thee Creator in the realm of the absolute, discussing, confessing and forgiving herself. Cleo turned to view Rastaland, seeing Layla and everyone as they should be, Layla swinging through lifetimes. Cleo relaxed in the shadowed sun's embrace, turning her full attention to being Earth's chaperone now that her niece was where she needed to be and Rastaland was at peace.

Isis and Layla, beings of the sun, conducted their eclipse ritual amongst the other sun beings. Layla was enthralled in her role, a star child, shape shifter, Thee Princess, Thee Empress, Thee Goddess, Thee Queen returned to her clan, now she's all things Rastaland.

On that day August twenty-first, two-thousand and seventeen around three pm Eastern time on Earth, when Thee Creator put the sun on dim and the moon beings glided between the sun and Earth, glimpsing the sun at that moment, you would have seen Layla's sun of soul dance! Her soul marks glistening in the sun's light.

And she lived happily, nappily, smokeily ever ever ever ever ever ever ever times eternity ever after!

The End Again!

INDEX A – CHARACTERS

Ras Fela: Creator of Rastaland, son of Osirus and Isis, brother to Layla. Ras Fela resides in his palace in Fela's Forrest, when he isn't roaming the universe. He is a shape shifter and fire being, has his own army The Panthers and speaks all languages.

Osirus: Father to Ras Fela and Layla, husband to Isis. Osirus resides in the City of Kings within the Truth Tower. He is a shape shifter, his army is the Rasta Renegades, he speaks LaRoz(the language of Rastaland), Dutch, English and Swahili.

Isis: Mother of Ras Fela and Layla, wife to Osirus. Isis resides in the City of Kings within the Truths Tower. Her city is called Tribe of Isis. She is a fire being who speaks LaRoz, Spanish, Dutch, English and Swahili. Cleo seer of Earth is her oldest sister, Boaz and Tapoah are her parents.

Winter: The middle sister of Isis, nemesis to Rastaland. A water being who dwells in the north of Rastaland. The Alligator Regulators, witches and demons, her allies. She loves to hate and hates to love.

Layla: Daughter of Osirus and Isis, sister to Ras Fela. Lost to Earth, she is a shape shifter and fire being…when she believes.

Hierba-Grass gnome and protector of Layla's Labyrinth .

Alligator Regulators – Some protect the King of Rastaland ; others protect The White Witch Winter.

Sun, Moon, Star, Angels, Humnoid Panthers, Ras Fox- Beings and protectors of Rastaland.

Reefa D- Exiled by Osirus , slave of Winter.

Marlaam- Guard of the Rasta Reformatory.

Index B - Definitions, Language & Cities

LaRoz - Main language of Rastaland, all beings speak LaRoz.

Ras Text - Rastaland Bible

Nema - Transports Beings of Rastaland back to any destination they prefer.

Raza - Transports someone else

Lomo - Transports you back to your previous destination when you time travel.

Beings - Rastaland is FULL of different beings as Earth is humans of diverse cultures, here are a few: Moon Beings, Sun Beings, Star Beings, Angels, Forrest Beings, Humanoid Lions, Panthers and Foxes. Air Beings and the Warwazi Beings.

Rasta Map - Seven Cities- Proffer, Daughter of Osirus, Ratsta Way, City of Kings, Tribe of Isis, Pallid and Fela's Forrest.

3 Lakes - Lake of Life in the Future Forrest.

Lake of Then in the Past Forrest.

Lake of Now in the Present Forrest.

1 River - Nile

1 Moon - La Luna

1 Sun - El Sol

1 Ocean - Africa

1 Island - Locks Island. Formed like an oval frisbee, touching Jupiter on it's right and Saturn on the left.

Life - Immortal, humanoid, King and Queen monarchy.

Atmosphere - Hot. Rastaland does not orbit the Sun, staying still absorbing heat and energy through its Sun.

INDEX C - LOCATIONS IN RASTALAND

Tree Park- one of the main parks of Rastaland.

    Rasta Baby Café- Local Cafe

    Lyrical Libations- library

    Community Center- Training and gathering place.

    Army Bases

    Rasta Reformatory- jail

    Black Mt. Rushmore- In Fela's Forrest.

    The Golden Temple- Sanctuary and portal to all spiritual realms.

Index D - Layla's Timeline

Expelled from Rastaland by Winter in 1693 on Earth, the Akhet moon cycle in Rastaland, she was in her seventh moon cycle or seven years old.

Layla had two lives on Earth that she was not visited by her family because they could not break the spell Winter had over her or reach her on Earth in 1717 and 1741.

1777- Cleo seer of Earth locates Layla on Earth in The Netherlands when she is seven years old.

This equaled three lives that Layla had on Earth, her family must retrieve her before her seventh life as an earthling.

1823- Layla is found by her father Osirus, living a life as a slave in Dar Es Salaam, Tanzania. This is their fourth attempt.

1937- Layla lives her fifth life in Paris, her family fails again to bring her home.

1957-Isis connects with Layla during her sixth life on Earth in Cuba.

2010- Ratsa Rabbit reaches Layla and brings her home, her families final time to try. Will she believe in herself enough to claim her rightful place?

INDEX E – BOOK CLUB DISCUSSION QUESTIONS

1. Have you heard or read any other literary work where the main characters were Black? Kings and Queens? If so which books?

2. What do you believe made Layla really believe in Rastaland and her abilities?

3. How does Winter compare to the obstacles we face in life? Do you believe in middle child syndrome?

4. Do you think Rastaland will have any more threats from beings or anything else in the future? If so what or whom?

5. Since Earth frustrated Layla, do you think she should leave Earth to her Creator and Aunt Cleo? Or continue casting 'good cop' spells? Why? Why not?

6. Do you agree with Layla's rant with the officers when she and Robert Rasta Rabbit were pulled over? Why? Why not?

7. If you could create a realm of your own, what would it be like? What did you like about Rastaland? What were your dislikes?

ABOUT THE AUTHOR

Iriel Sayeed is a professional performing poet who resides in her home town of Cincinnati, Ohio.

She has performed poetry all over the world; New York, California, Chicago, Africa, and Amsterdam to name a few.

Author of two books of poetry; "Coming Into Consciousness" and "Iriellic Illusions", this is her first novel.

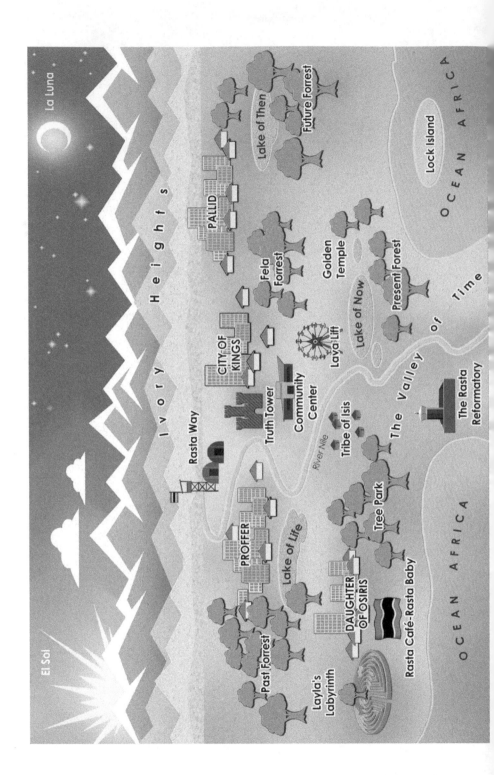